Finding Closure

By

Larry Webb

Special thanks to Dr. Mary Anna Kruch who edits my works and offers many helpful ideas to make the story flow smoother, and hopefully, the book read better for the reader.

Check out my web site at: www.larrywebb-author.com

Finding Closure
By
Larry Webb

Chapter 1

After Madelyn and Jay's two sons, Ryan and Rayden, closed the door to their bedroom for the night, Maddie got out of her loveseat, walked across the living room, and sat down beside her husband. "OK, Jayden, let's hear it. What did those DNA results reveal?"

He smiled and slid closer so he could drape his arm over her shoulder. "Oh, yeah, the report's still in my pocket. I haven't looked at it yet—been half afraid of what we're going to find out. Besides, I've been waiting for the boys to go to bed. So, I guess maybe now we should take a look?"

"Yes, it's been driving me nuts. Seems like I've been waiting all day. Open it."

"Madelyn, before we take a look, can we talk?"

"Sure, Honey. What's on your mind?"

Jayden scrunched up tighter with Madelyn and stared off into space before answering. "I'm not sure if I even want to see what it says."

"Sure you do. Think of all the stress you've gone through to get them. After your father died, you talked Mrs. Miller into giving you the pipe he had in his mouth when he passed for a *keepsake*—which was quite a line of bologna in itself. Incidentally, I've always loved the story about when you were a kid and referred to his pipe as his binky behind his back, because he always had it stuffed into his mouth?

"Anyway, after she gave the thing to you, you had it tested at the forensics lab at State. So, you may as well open the package and read the report. And also keep in mind, you haven't considered John Miller to be your father for years, so whichever way it goes, it really doesn't matter. Let's find out right now—together."

"Madelyn, it's not just that. Something else has been crawling like a worm through my brain. Have you thought about the fact that Ryan is fifteen? That's how old I was when I crept out of the place on my hands and knees and moved in with Mom and Rob. The age similarities here are freaky. I swear, I couldn't handle it if one of our boys ran away and never came back."

"Jay, there are *no* similarities here. Just because Ryan is the same age you were when it happened, is irrelevant. You lived with a cruel, heartless father figure and a mother who cowered in fear for her own safety. And, to top it off, instead of protecting you, she sacrificed her only child because of it. Our boys have the most loving, kind, and gentle home life anyone could ask for. Both are happy, well-adjusted kids. So, what's your point?"

"I don't know," Jayden said. "I guess I still haven't gotten over the fact that the boys learned about a grandfather they never knew existed from a friend of theirs who offered condolences at school after he died. And, then having them sneak around behind our backs to find his grave."

"I know, I wasn't happy with that either," Madelyn said. "We should have told them about the Millers a long time ago."

"I think what's maybe even worse was to have Rayden build up such a hatred for the man, that he smashed his fist into the Miller headstone so hard he dislocated three knuckles. And to top it off, do you have any idea how it made me feel to have our sons show us my father's grave on the way home from Rayden's visit to the Urgent Care, because I didn't even know what cemetery he was buried in?

"And, what about the fact that later on the boys snooped around and found their grandmother, making it necessary for our family to reconnect with my biological mother after twenty-five years—something I had no intention of doing?

"I know what you're saying," Madelyn said. "But, I think there's something else I'm more concerned about. I've never been happy about of all those childhood secrets you've kept from them their whole lives—things we knew they'd probably learn about someday. Well, now those things are coming back to haunt you, aren't they?"

"I know, and I agree with you, I should have told them about my biological parents long ago."

"To think, they've learned about all of this stuff at pretty much the same time. For instance, what had to be going through their minds when they found out that Grandma Roberts and Uncle Rob are more 'adoptive' type relatives than biological?"

"We should have let out the truth bit-by-bit over the years."

"What might even be worse is the fact that you and Rob both bailed out and suckered Mom Roberts into telling them about all the abuse that she knew of. Not only that, she also had to tell them all the information regarding the family relationships."

"I'm not proud of that, either. I think it probably makes us both look like cowards in the kids' eyes."

"No it doesn't, but *you* are the one who is going to have to deal with this DNA test. Are you going to tell them—whatever it reveals?"

"Yes, I will. I have to," Jayden said. "I cannot keep any more secrets from them. It's just that thinking about what the results might show freaks me out. Over the years, I've convinced myself that he wasn't—he couldn't be my real father. No biological parent could be like him, but what if he was? What happens if he was my actual, biological father? What if he wasn't?"

"It doesn't matter anymore. He's dead. Either way, you've got to tell the boys. In the meantime, it's time to quit stalling. Open the package and let's see what it says."

Jayden slid his arm off of Madelyn's shoulder, reached into his pocket, and pulled out the small package. He turned it over a couple of times, looking at it. Then he took a deep breath, smiled at Madelyn, and opened the envelope attached to the parcel containing the pipe.

He silently read the single page report. When he finished, he passed it over to his wife without saying a word.

After reading it, Madelyn handed it back. "You were right all along. That man was *not* your father after all. I wonder who was? Do you think your mother even knows at this point, and can or will tell you?"

"Hard telling. Who knows what's going on in her head any more? This is crazy. Was she messing around on the old man? Did she get impregnated by a sperm donor? Was I adopted and they never told me? In her state of mind, do I dare even ask her?"

"Honey, I don't know. Her dementia has taken a serious toll on her memory, disposition, and everything else. Like we've been talking about lately, it seems like the situation keeps getting worse all the time," Madelyn said. "She babbles incoherently more and more often these days especially when she's flustered."

"I know," Jayden said. "And, yet, there are times when she acts somewhat normal. Guess we'll have to wait and see what way it's going to be when I confront her. In the meantime, what and when do I tell the boys about this?"

"Let's hold off on telling them anything for right now. I know, you can't keep it a secret too much longer, but let's not rush into it," Madelyn said. "Wait until you've had a chance to talk to Mrs. Miller. You know the boys will drive both of us nuts if we can't give them all the facts at once."

"What I do know for sure is, I've gotta tell Rob and Mom Roberts. After that, I don't know. My head is full of more questions than answers."

"Yes, you definitely have to tell your big brother. He's been your protector and body guard for the past twenty-five years. You need to tell him right away—Mom Roberts too. After that, I don't know how we're going to handle things. Guess we'll have to see what those two have to say and go from there."

10

Jay pulled the phone out of his pocket and looked at it. "Should I call Rob now?"

"Sure," Madelyn said. "See if you can get him to come over tonight without his kids."

"They ought to be in bed by now anyway."

Jay punched in #5 on his speed dial and waited.

After a couple rings, Rob answered. "CIA Assassination Squad. Where would you like us to dispose of your body? We *always* recommend the *Dead Sea*."

"Bob Bob, do you ever get serious?"

"Not when I know I'm talking to you. What do you want, little bro? It's after nine. It's past your bedtime. Why aren't you asleep?"

Looking over at Madelyn, Jayden grinned, rolled his eyes, and slowly shook his head. Then he spoke to his brother, trying not to laugh. "Any chance you could slip out of the house and come over here *alone* for a couple of minutes? I've got something to show you and need your input."

"Sounds important," Rob said, suddenly serious.

"It is."

"Be right there."

11

While they waited, Madelyn made her way out to the kitchen. "I've got to brew a quick pot of coffee. As we well know, Rob manages much better when he's loaded up on caffeine. We won't tell him it's decaf."

How many times had she and Jay chuckled, wondering how Rob ever functioned on those rare occasions when he had to go to court—without his hand wrapped around a cup of coffee? As a senior partner in a corporate law firm, he didn't spend too much time in front of a judge, but there were times.

During the early days, Rob and Jay referred to their relationship as "adoptive/pseudo-step brothers." Since then, they've always been just plain *brothers*. These days, they and their mom, Jane Roberts, lived in a triangle, none further than two blocks from the other, it wouldn't take Rob long to get there.

Five minutes later he walked through the front door. "Hey Bro, what's up?"

Madelyn ambled back into the living room and handed him his coffee—before he even had a chance to sit down. "Sorry, I don't have any cookies," she said. "The boys inhaled what was left tonight before going to bed."

"Simple solution to that problem," Rob said, managing to keep a straight face. "Wake the little dudes up and march them right down here so they can stir up a fresh batch."

"Yeah, right, that'd work real well," Madelyn laughed.

"So, why did you interrupt my peaceful evening serenity, after I'd safely strapped my own adolescent monsters into their straitjackets and padlocked them to their beds?"

"This came in the mail today," Jayden said, smiling at his brother's wisecrack. Rob's boys were as loved and spoiled as his own. He handed the letter to Rob. "Wanted you to have a look before Maddie and I take the next step—as if we even know what the next step is going to be. That's why we dragged your butt off your cozy sofa and made you come over."

Rob took a moment and read the entire report. Without a word, he looked back and forth between Jayden and Madelyn, and then scanned the document a second time before speaking. "It doesn't surprise me one bit. I've never believed that a *real* father could beat the living crap out of his own kid nightly just to let off steam after fighting with his wife—to say nothing about the fact that he kicked him hard enough to break two ribs. Actually, I almost feel relieved. So, have you told the boys yet? What'd they say?"

"No," Jayden said. "So, don't tell yours right away either. That's one of the reasons why we called you. Not sure how we want to handle this thing. I know we'll tell Mom Roberts tomorrow, but do I tell my biological mother? You know how fast she's been going downhill mentally lately. However, like we were talking before you got here, there are moments when she's more lucid than others. Will she even remember any of this? What do I do, Rob?"

"Well, if you want my honest opinion, I agree, I wouldn't tell the kids yet either. Mom? Yes. She's been with you every step of the way. Besides, sometimes I think she's more level-headed under duress than either one of us. Why don't the two of you go over there right now? I'll stay here and babysit until you get back just in case somebody wakes up."

"You think it'll freak her out with us going over there this time of night?" Jayden asked.

"No, go ahead. Get going. I'll call and give her a heads up. That is, after I refill my cup. You sure those characters ate all the cookies?"

When Jay and Madelyn pulled into Mom Robert's driveway, they noticed she'd already turned on the porch light. The two of them walked in, got their hugs, and sat down on the sofa across from her. Without any of the normal chit-chat, Jayden pulled the document out of his pocket and handed it to her.

"Need you to read this. Then we'll talk," he said.

She looked at him and then Madelyn before taking the sheet of paper out of the envelope. She read it in silence. When she finished, she refolded it, replaced it into its packet, and passed it back to him. "Wow! Brings up a bunch of questions, doesn't it? What are you going to do with this information?"

"That's one of the reasons why we're here. What do *you* think we should do with this? When do we tell the boys? We have to somewhere along the way. Like Maddie and I discussed, do I confront my mother first? In her state of mind, will she even know? Does my biological father, whoever he is, even know I exist? If he does, why have we never been in any kind of contact—or, have we, and I didn't know because nobody ever clued me in?"

Madelyn looked back and forth between Mom Roberts and Jayden. "I'm thinking you can forget that one. As evil as John Miller was, I don't think he would have ever allowed any contact between you and your biological father to happen with his knowledge—that is, if he even knew about the other man. Unless, of course, he was looking for something like child support. Then I could see the possibility."

"Wouldn't it be wild if my mother had somehow managed to have my biological father and I meet without him, the old man, or me knowing it? I always thought she was kind of sneaky. I think something like that would have been just like her."

"So, when did your parents get married?" Mom Roberts asked. "Any chance it happened while she was pregnant with you or after you were born? Could she have been married to or dating your biological father first?"

"Hadn't thought of that," Jayden said. "I guess the next step is to talk to her and hope she's having a good day. If she's having one of her more and more frequently bad ones, she won't know anything anyway.

"In the meantime, Mom, what about the boys? I'm worried about them and won't withhold the truth from them forever. It wouldn't be right. Especially, because of the way Rayden thinks he hates the man. It really messes with my mind, thinking about how my son absolutely abhors a grandfather he's never even met."

"Yes he does, and you know why. Anyway, hold off on letting them in on it," Mom Roberts said. "That can wait until you have more information. Telling the boys now without knowing all the details might drive them a tad berserk—and, let's face it, my grandsons are loopy enough as it is. I think your next step is to go talk to Mrs. Miller and see if you can find out anything from her."

Chapter 2

The next afternoon after lunch, Jayden left his job as
director of the university's rare-isotope lab and drove over to
his biological mother's home. After he rang the doorbell, he
watched the window as she pulled back the curtain and peeked
out at him before coming to the door. Smiling, he thought to
himself, *some things never change.*

"You're supposed to be working," she said when she
opened the door. "What brings me the pleasure this beautiful
afternoon?"

She unhooked both chains and pushed open the screen
door. No hugs passed between them.

"I'm doing some research for a family historical biography
I'm writing for the boys when they get a little older and need
more information about you, John and my early years. Do you

have your marriage certificate handy? I need some data off of it."

Mrs. Miller frowned. "You still won't refer to him as your father, will you, even now that he's dead and buried?"

"Nope. You still have that metal file cabinet where you used to keep all your records? It's probably in there."

"Yeah, I guess. Don't even know where it is though. I wanted to dust the top of it one day, but couldn't find it. You know, things do get a little grimy when you don't use them. Maybe I should pull it out into the living room so I can use it. That way I could make sure it gets dusted regularly."

"Uh, yeah. Mind if I look in my old bedroom closet? That's where you used to keep it. I can't imagine you've moved it."

Without waiting for an answer, Jayden walked up the steps to his old room. Looking around, the place appeared as dingy and unwelcoming to him as it had the day he walked out of it for the last time twenty-five years ago. He slid open the closet door and spotted the file cabinet—that and some of his old clothes still hanging on the rod. There were items he'd intentionally left the afternoon he and Rob had sneaked over and emptied the place of all his wanted belongings—before depositing his front door key at his place on the dining room table, swearing to Rob he'd never come back.

He looked at the ugly, yellow sweater John had bought him for Christmas the year before he left. He had hated it so much, he only wore it once. He wondered if either of his parents had ever even noticed—he'd bet they hadn't.

He pulled open the top cabinet and began his search. After a short time, he found their marriage license. He checked the dates. They had been married a year and a half when he was born. So much for any prior marriage birth, he thought. That meant either she had an affair, sperm donor, or they adopted him. Which one was it?

Jayden walked back down to the living room where his mother sat, humming to herself.

"Oh, hi," she said, looking up surprised. "When did you get here? I was thinking about you just the other day. Haven't seen you lately."

"Uh, yes. I've been here for close to a half hour—upstairs looking at your marriage license, and I've got some questions."

"Oh, yes. It's up there in your old bedroom—in the closet. Why, are you planning to get married?"

"Maddie and I have been married for almost seventeen years. I'm wondering about something to do with you and John. Do you remember the pipe of his you gave me after he died? The one you said he had in his mouth when he took his last breath?"

"Pipe? What would he be doing with a pipe in his mouth? He wasn't a plumber."

"The old Meerschaum pipe he smoked for years. Anyway, I had a DNA test run from it. John Miller was *not* my biological father. Who was? It wasn't him, so don't try to tell me otherwise. It was somebody else, and you never told me? Why?" Where did I come from? Who was responsible for my birth?"

Mrs. Miller looked at him, with a very strange expression on her face before answering. "I bought you. I thought you knew that."

"What?" Jayden said. "What do you mean, you bought me?"

"We were living in Florida at the time and in the process of moving here for your dad's new job at General Motors. We were packed and ready to go. The afternoon before we left, I met a man at a bus stop and struck up a conversation with him. I was crying and feeling sorry for myself, and he asked me what the problem was. I told him I wanted a new baby, and your father wanted nothing to do with the idea."

She paused, as if that were the end of the story.

"Well, go on," Jayden said. "Then what happened?"

"He made me a deal. He said if I promised to get out of town immediately, he would sell me his kid for a thousand dollars."

"His kid? He said he'd sell you his kid?"

"Yep, that's what he said. He told me you belonged to him and were for sale."

"What a nut case. You mean you actually bought into that scheme?"

"Oh, he was a very nice man—so understanding, so kind to me."

"Yeah, right. Sounds like a real winner. So, if that was the case, and you wanted a child so badly, why didn't you adopt one legally?" Jayden asked.

Looking somewhat blankly, Mrs. Miller continued with her side of the story. "Well, let's face it. Buying you that way was a lot cheaper, easier, and faster than going through some adoption agency. Those places are a pain in the neck."

"Where'd you get the money? You guys never had any when I wanted or needed something. Besides, if you were moving from Florida to Michigan for a new job, there probably wouldn't be a whole lot of extra cash lying around."

"Oh, that was no big deal. Your sneaky father had saved up a bunch of money for a golf outing, which, as it ended up, he couldn't go to because of our sudden move. So, the next morning after I talked to the sweet man who wanted to sell you, I swiped the money from where your dad thought he had it hidden and met the guy again at the park. That's when I bought you.

"Two hours later, the three of us left for Michigan. Your father was *not* happy. He never forgave me or you. That's one reason why he never particularly liked or accepted you. It had taken him a long time to save all that money, and he thought I blew it when I spent it all buying some kid. We fought about it for years—at least until you ran away from home. Then we quit arguing about it, and our lives smoothed out."

"Was he the angriest because you stole his money or because you bought me?" Jayden asked.

"I don't know. Hold on a minute. I've got to get a glass of water. All this talking has made my throat dry."

She stood and went into the kitchen. After getting her drink, she walked back into the living room.

She looked at Jayden with another somewhat blank look. "Did you dust the file cabinet while you were up there? I bet it really needs it. So, when did you get here? I haven't seen you in ages. Did you find my marriage certificate? If you're gonna get married, you have to get your own—you can't use mine."

Jayden stood and told her goodbye. He walked out the door without another word.

• • •

Jayden didn't know what to think. He had confronted his mother about John Miller not being his biological father, and she talked gibberish until he left. The only thing that made any sense at all was her proclamation about buying him from someone at a park. *Could he have been a victim of some kind of human trafficking operation?*

Thinking of that possibility brought up another concern for him. He suddenly remembered he'd never seen his original birth certificate either. All he had was a photo copy Mrs. Miller had given to Mom Roberts. He had needed one when he signed up for driver's training. He ended up using the same document for his college application, social security number, marriage license, and passport.

He made a quick u-turn and went back to Mrs. Miller's. Like before, she did her creepy peering out from behind the curtains routine before opening the door.

"Hi, Jay," she said sounding happy to see him. "Haven't seen you in ages. What's up?"

"I would like to check the file cabinet again for something else. I need my original birth certificate. I assume you must have it up there with all your other papers."

"You don't have a birth certificate. Didn't I ever tell you? I bought you at a real estate auction, you and the encyclopedias at the same time. I got a real deal by taking both of you—sort of like a two-for-one sale. You, of all people, should know auctioneers don't give out official documents like that at estate sales. You wouldn't expect to get a warranty for a used bike at one, would you? After somebody buys something, they just move on to the next item. If I remember right, I think a corner cabinet came up right after I bought you. I almost bid on it."

Jayden smiled. He didn't even bother to remind her of the replica she'd given Mom Roberts years previously. He told her he still needed to take a look just in case. After all, the *auctioneer might* have given her a copy that she'd forgotten about. He spent another half hour going through every file in the cabinet. Nothing.

Then, as he was about ready to quit looking, something caught his eye—an old grimy envelope in the bottom of one of the folders with his name on it. He folded back the flap and pulled out the sheet of paper in it. The top line of the document read, *Certificate of Death.* He examined it. Jayden Scott Miller had died two months after his birth of Sudden Infant Death Syndrome. (SIDS)

Open mouthed and staring, Jayden carried the paper down to the living room where his mother sat looking at a magazine turned upside down.

He glared at her before speaking, not really knowing what to say. "What is the deal with this thing? This certified

26

document in my hand says I died of SIDS when I was two months old. I'm still here. Tell me, what is *this* all about?"

Mrs. Miller set down her magazine beside her, and her eyes blurred with tears. "You did. Your father was taking care of you one afternoon while I had gone shopping. Seems like you got fussy, so he laid you down on your belly for a nap in your crib, walked out, and closed the door. When I came home from the store, I checked up on you and found you dead. Your father never forgave himself. He loved you to pieces."

"You're not making any sense. I couldn't be dead for two months and then have you suddenly *buy me from somebody*. It doesn't work that way."

Mrs. Miller's dried her eyes with a tissue, and then spoke with more clarity than she had in some time. "The *original* Jayden died of SIDS at two months. Then, two months after his death, I met a man in a park. I was sitting on a bench, crying over the death of my baby and the fact I would be leaving his body behind in a cemetery when we moved. I told the man I was afraid I'd never see his burial place again—and I haven't. The man sat down beside me and comforted me. Then, he gave me a chance to replace my dead son."

"So, you really did buy me from some stranger?"

"Yes, after I picked you up the next day from the guy, *you* became Jayden. I can honestly say, I don't know where you came from. I didn't care then and I don't now. The sad part is, your father couldn't or wouldn't accept you. He didn't want you. He wanted me to take you back. I thought at the time he just wanted his money back. I wouldn't do it. He told me he was afraid he'd accidentally kill you again. However, I got my way, and we left Florida. We drove straight through to Michigan for your dad's new job, arguing the whole way with me carrying you in my arms. End of story."

"OK, one more question," Jayden said. "Whatever happened to my original birth certificate? Like I told you when I first got here is, all I have is the copy you gave Mom Roberts after I left this place."

"After I gave a copy of it to Mrs. Roberts, I told your dad about her asking for it. He had a little temper tantrum and then shredded the original. He said the real Jayden was dead, and you were finally out of our lives, so we didn't need the thing anymore."

And that ended her moment of clarity. From then on, the conversation made no sense, and Jayden couldn't bring her back to reality. Finally, he gave up and stood to leave. When he did, Mrs. Miller told him how much she'd enjoyed his visit. It was the first time they'd had a chance to sit down and talk without all those other people hanging around and listening in to their conversation. As he walked out the door, she asked for the second time, "Who did you say those kids are at your house?"

Chapter 3

Jayden drove around for a half hour or so trying to digest the latest. *Was it true? Was there really an original Jayden Miller who had died, and he had taken the baby's place through some kind of child trafficking scam? Jayden Miller's death certificate indicated that might have been the case.* His mind raced all over the place. By the time he arrived home, Madelyn had already begun getting dinner around. The boys were still at soccer practice, so it was just the two of them.

Jay jogged from the garage into the house. He looked around. "Where are the boys?"

"At practice, Honey. They're not here. What's going on? You look like you've seen a ghost." Madelyn turned off the stove, took Jayden by the arm, and led him into the living room and the two sat down together on the sofa.

His face blanched, and he looked her in the eye. "Maybe you're the one who's seen one. You are *not* going to believe this tale, and I have no clue as to what is fact and what is fantasy."

"Tell me," Madelyn said. "What's going on? You look half freaked out. Tell me everything."

"After I found their marriage certificate, I looked at it and found they had been married for a year and a half by the time I was born. When I came back down stairs, I told her about the DNA test and asked her who my real father was. Are you ready for this? At first, all I got was a satanic laugh and weird look. Then she settled down and told me a story about how she bought me from some guy at a park for $1,000."

"What? She said she *bought* you from somebody?"

"Yes, but that isn't the weirdest part," Jayden said. "It gets better. "After I left, I remembered I'd wanted to find my own birth certificate, so went back and took a look. Here's where it gets really dicey."

"Will you quit beating around the bush," Madelyn said, smirking. "What'd you find out then?"

"What'd I find? Guess. Take a wild stab in the dark. Here's betting you won't even come close."

"I have no idea, Honey. Tell me."

"My death certificate."

"Your what? That's crazy," Madelyn said. "You went over to find their marriage certificate and then your birth certificate, and end up finding your own death certificate? Quick, give me all the details before the boys get home."

Concerned and full of questions, for Jayden's sake, Madelyn tried to keep as calm and low key as possible. He didn't need to see her spooking out like he had—regardless of how she felt inside. "So, let's make sure I've got this straight. When you first got there, you did find the marriage certificate and found out they'd been married a while when you were born. So, then you told her about the DNA test, she said she bought you. Wow!"

"Yeah, crazy, huh? Ever have one of those days when so much weird was going on, you have no idea how you're feeling—giddy, squirrely, nerved up? That's been me for the past hour or so. Anyway, that was her story when I first got there. Then, like I told you before, after I left the place, that's when it popped into my head that I've never seen my original birth certificate. All I've ever had was a copy. So, I drove around the block and went back to see if I could find it."

What she'd say when you walked back in after leaving less than five minutes before?" Madelyn said.

"At that point, she'd completely forgotten I'd been there. When I asked her about the document, she said I didn't have one because she'd bought me at an estate sale. I went back up to my old bedroom and searched the file cabinet again. There was no sign of a birth certificate –just my death certificate. "

"So, what did you do when you found it?"

"I went back down and asked her again," Jayden said. "This time she switched the story back again, telling me she bought me from some guy at a park."

"An estate sale? Some guy at a park? Wonder what the truth is. The sad thing is, we'll probably never know."

"I know, so here we are with different versions of pretty much the same story—each saying she bought me for a thousand dollars."

Jayden spent the next few minutes relating to Madelyn all the details of the two different visits.

"So, the only thing consistent in her confusion was the fact that she'd paid a thousand dollars cash for you. I wonder if there's any truth to the story at all?"

"I don't know. Mentally, she was all over the place most of the time. I think this is the worse I've ever seen her," Jayden said. "However, I wonder if dredging up the past triggered something and made her semi-lucid for a short time."

"I don't like the sounds of this," Madelyn said. "We've known for a while that her mind is going, but it's beginning to sound like maybe she's lost it completely. Do you think she's safe staying there by herself? I don't really want her living with us either. The boys tend to feel real uncomfortable when she's around—especially Rayden. What are we going to do?"

"At this point, I don't think we have a choice. She's completely oblivious to anything resembling reality. She even wanted to know who all those kids are we have hanging around here. I don't trust her. In this condition she's apt to go wandering off someplace and get lost. Who knows what would happen then? I don't want her living here either, but I don't want her hurting herself. Anyway, I think we need to find an assisted living facility as soon as possible."

"What about the boys?" Madelyn asked. "Do you think it's time to clue them in on what's going on? After all, you did promise not to keep any secrets from them in the future when they found about Mr. Miller dying from a friend at school. Nothing like getting condolences for a grandfather you didn't even know existed. I really did feel sorry for them finding out that way."

Jay looked at her and smiled; his mind obviously at work again. "I agree, and, you know what? I think maybe we can use one of the boys to help resolve another one of my relatively new questions."

"Oh, oh, what do you have you have up your sleeve this time?"

"You know how she's always bumming gum from the boys? She did the same thing from me when I was a kid. Let's have her over for dinner and get one of the boys to give her a stick of gum, and then when she sticks it under her plate like she always does during dinner, one of us can snag it afterwards, slip it into a freezer bag and get another DNA analysis. After everything that happened today, I'm even more and more certain she's *not* my biological mother either."

Dinner that night took longer than normal. Jayden's family had a number of things to discuss. For the first time, he told the boys about his acquisition of Grandpa Miller's Meerschaum pipe and the DNA test he'd had run on it at the university. Then he lowered his head, raised his eye brows and stared at his youngest. "Rayden, when I tell you the next piece of news, there'll be no jumping up and down and cheering. Got it?"

Suddenly wary about why he'd been singled out—and his dad's tone of voice, Rayden set his fork down on the table, and folded his hands in his lap. He was all ears.

"The DNA test confirmed one of my long-time suspicions. John Miller was NOT my biological father or *your* grandfather. I talked to Grandma Miller about it and got two different stories—both indicating that she had bought me from some stranger. "

"Dad, I'm *not* going to cheer," Rayden said, flushing a tinge of red. "I don't know if she bought you or not, and I don't care. Almost hope she did. No real father or mother would *ever* treat their own kid the way they did you. I can't say I'm happy and want to cheer about it, but I think I'm relieved to know he wasn't."

"Dad, are you willing and able to tell us what she told you?" Ryan asked softly. "You said she gave you two different versions about *buying* you. Can you tell us the story?"

Jayden knew the boys were soft-pedaling around his feelings and emotions. He loved it. He loved them. He smiled, and, then went on and related the entire story, including the part about the death certificate. He also let his boys know, he felt confident that neither one of the Millers could possibly be his biological parent.

As the boys digested that part of the story, he told them about his and their mom's discussion that afternoon about getting Grandma Miller into some kind of assisted care facility. She was no longer safe living alone.

Still choosing his words carefully, Rayden looked tenderly at his dad and asked, "So, you don't think she's your real mother either?"

"No, after today, I really don't. However, we're gonna find out for sure," Jayden said.

37

He went on and told them the plan he'd discussed with their mother that afternoon and how they intended to make it work. They'd invite Grandma Miller over for dinner some night in the next couple of days, and before they ate, both boys would pop gum into their mouths at the same time, and the plot would go on from there.

That Saturday the family sat around the living room waiting for dinner to finish cooking when Ryan pulled a pack of gum out of his pocket. He nonchalantly un-wrapped a piece and slipped it into his mouth.

"Me too," Rayden said, holding out his hand.

Ryan took one out of the pack and tossed it to his brother. He casually glanced over and saw Grandma Miller glaring at him.

Suddenly she snarled. "Jayden Scott Miller, you bring me a stick of that gum, *now*!

Struggling not to laugh, Ryan pulled one out of the pack and walked over and handed it to her. "Uh, I'm Ryan, not Jayden."

Jayden cleared his throat loudly enough to get Ryan's attention. When he turned his head and looked at his dad, Jay very slightly shook his head.

Ryan nodded once without speaking. He stood there a moment until she took the wrapper off her gum. When she handed him the paper, he took it to the basket.

For the rest of the day, every time she spoke to either one of the boys, she would call him Jayden. And each time, her tone appeared to them a bit rougher than it was when she spoke to their parents.

After dinner, while clearing the table, Madelyn carefully scraped the gum off the bottom of the dinner plate with a knife and slipped it into a quart sized freezer bag, making sure she didn't touch it. They wanted no one's DNA on the gum but Grandma Miller's.

"Honey," Madelyn said to Ryan barely above a whisper. "Sneak this out and put it into the refrigerator, would you please?" Both boys had been helping with the cleanup, and he just happened to be the closest to her when she bagged the gum.

Chapter 4

The next few days were hectic. Madelyn used her nursing expertise to find the appropriate doctor to evaluate Mrs. Miller. The geriatric specialist recommended immediate placement in an assisted living facility. Her physical health and cognitive functioning had deteriorated much more rapidly and severely than Jay and Madelyn had realized. The doctor indicated she was in an unstable and unsafe condition to live alone anymore.

In less than a week they had her placed where she would be safe, protected, and provided for. To her delight, she didn't have to worry anymore about cooking, shopping, or cleaning. She loved it. She quickly befriended three other ladies who were all suffering from the same ailment. Their dinnertime conversations were very interesting to any bystanders. They all talked at once about four or more different topics without any of them realizing it.

A week later, Jayden had the results of the latest DNA test from the campus lab. As he had suspicioned, Mrs. Miller was *not* his biological mother. Now, what? Who was? Was the crazy child trafficking story true?

"What do you think, Madelyn? Should I try to confront her again? She won't remember our other discussions, I'm sure. Will anything click in her head, or will she think I'm the custodian again like she did a couple of days ago?"

"Honey, you don't have a choice," Madelyn said. "You have to go see her and ask. If she's having a good day, she might be able to tell you something useful. If not, she won't— plain and simple."

The next afternoon, Jayden went to visit the woman he grew up thinking was his mother. Anxiety was only a small part of what he felt.

He caught up with her in her room, looking at a magazine. Jayden smiled. Growing up, he had never seen her read anything other than the children's books she read to him when he was a toddler. After he started correcting her when she misread something, she refused to read to him anymore, and he never saw her read anything else for her own pleasure.

He sat down in the chair across from her. When she looked up with a rather blank look on her face, he wasn't sure if she recognized him or not. Still, he had to tell her what was on his mind. "I've had a DNA test run, checking on my parental background. According to the results, you are *not* my biological mother. Who is? Do you know?"

"Of course I don't. I've always told you I bought you from a door-to-door vacuum cleaner salesman for a thousand dollars. I used money your dad had saved up for the down payment on a new car. Oh, was he ever ticked. He never forgave me or you. So, how would I ever know who your real mother is? C'mon, use your head for a change."

"Uh, are you sure you have no idea?" Jayden said. "You've told me three times now that you bought me for a thousand dollars from three different people. I want to know where I came from and how you happened to have me."

"Hey, that's not even important. What is essential right now is for you to tell me something. I want to know when you are going to settle down, get a job, and get married. Have you ever considered one of the local factories like your dad did? They're always hiring people like you. You did finish your GED, didn't you? You know, Roger, I'm not getting any younger. I do need grand kids. I want a darling little baby to cuddle again just like I did when I bought you. You do like girls don't you? Are you dating anyone?"

Smiling, Jayden couldn't help himself. He pulled out his phone and showed her the pictures of the boys. "Speaking of grandkids, do these two look at all familiar to you?"

"Yeah, those are the groundskeepers you hired to take care of the mansion. They don't count. I want cuddly little grandbabies."

• • •

Finding out Mrs. Miller was not his biological mother had not come as a huge shock to Jayden. Naturally, it left him with all kinds of questions. Who were his biological parents, and what had happened? How did he ever end up in the hands of people who didn't even want him?

Knowing the whole thing was weighing mightily on him, Madelyn had a suggestion. "Jay, why don't you do one of those commercial DNA tests to see what it comes up with? It may not answer any of our questions, but what can it hurt? All you have to do is spit in a test tube and send it in. From what I've heard, they are pretty accurate with ancestry origins anyway. If nothing else, it might be kind of fun to see what part of the world your ancestors came from."

"If I do, I think all four of us should. It would be interesting to see how the boys and I differ because of your genes. We kind of know about yours. On your mother's side you had the Mayflower, and on your dad's, they traveled from England to New York and then migrated west. It'll be fun comparing and contrasting."

That night at the dinner table, Jayden asked the boys what they thought of the idea.

"Yeah, yeah, Dad, let's do it," Rayden spurted. After wiping the slobber off his mouth with his sleeve, he continued. "There've been a whole bunch of the guys at school who've done it. Lots of fun seeing how things go when moms and dads' genes get all mixed up in the kids' bloodlines."

"Yeah," Ryan said. "They're really accurate too. Like, two brothers or a sister and a brother will come out almost exactly the same."

So, after dinner Jayden ordered the test kits on line and they waited. It seemed like it took forever for them to come in the mail.

When they finally arrived, Jayden read the directions as the family gathered around. "Okay, here's what we're going to do. Tonight before bedtime after no one has had anything to eat or drink for an hour or so, we'll do it together."

The time finally came. Laughing uproariously, the foursome stood in a circle, and spit into their tubes up to the designated line. Immediately afterwards, it was a bowl of cereal and then off to bed for the boys.

A week after sending in the tubes, a phone call on the house phone interrupted their dinner. All their cell phones were turned off and in a basket on the counter. Jayden and Madelyn looked at each other with wrinkled brows. No one who knew them called during their dinner hour. Knowing darned well it was a robo-call, Jayden still checked caller ID. When he saw who it was, he picked up the phone, answered, and listened. Then he wandered off into the living room out of earshot of the family. Madelyn and the boys looked at each other with frowns. That wasn't like him at all. What was going on?

A minute or two later, Jayden walked back into the kitchen and put the phone back in its place. "I've gotta go. That was the assisted care facility. They've taken my mother to the hospital. They're thinking she's stroked out. Doesn't sound good."

"I'm going with you. Boys, you're on duty. Clean up after you finish eating. We'll be back when we get back. Behave yourselves and get to bed on time," Madelyn said.

"Don't worry about us, Mom. We'll be fine. And, you *don't* have to call Uncle Rob to come babysit us. We *can* take care of ourselves," Rayden said.

When Jay and Madelyn arrived at the emergency room, the policeman at the door asked them for identification and why they were there.

"My mother, Mrs. Miller, was brought in from her assisted care facility. They told me on the phone she might have had a stroke."

"Follow me," he said after double checking the name on Jayden's license. He hustled them through security and had his assistant escort them to Mrs. Miller's room.

No one was with her when they walked in, but she was attached to multiple machines. The EKG, blood pressure, and pulse rates were obvious. Jayden had no clue what the rest of them were.

Madelyn didn't comment on any of the devices. As a nurse, she had, by habit, looked and knew exactly what she was looking at.

Jayden put his hand on his mother's wrist. It felt cool to the touch. She never moved.

A short time later an emergency room doctor came in and introduced himself. "Dr. Miller, the news is not good. Your mother's brain function is dead, and her body is being kept alive by the machines. We need you to make a decision."

The hospital held copies of the records from the assisted care facility, and the doctor knew Jayden had the medical power of attorney.

"So, what are our options?" Jayden asked.

After a brief discussion, Jayden made the decision no one ever wants to make, and the medical doctor removed life support. A short time later, she took her last breath.

Within two hours of their arrival, Mrs. Miller had passed and arrangements had been made to send her to one of the local funeral homes. By the time Jay and Madelyn returned home, both boys had showered and were in their pajamas, ready for bed.

One look at their parents' faces and both boys knew. They wrapped their arms around their dad and didn't say a word. They didn't need to. Jayden and Madelyn then confirmed what the boys had assumed. Knowing they should leave Mom and Dad to cope, the boys went to bed without being told.

The next several days were even more hectic than normal. There were all the preparations for the funeral, visitation, and then the actual service. Afterwards, the combined Miller and

Roberts family and several friends gathered at the cemetery for the internment.

Standing back and watching the last rites, Grandma Roberts focused her attention on Rayden. He was the more emotional of Jayden's two boys and by far the biggest spitfire—to say nothing of the fact that he was the most classic *daddy's boy* she had ever seen. She watched as Ray kept looking back and forth between his dad and the Miller headstone—the one he had slammed his fist into, dislocating several knuckles months before, when he and his brother first learned of their abusive grandfather and his passing. When Ray looked at the headstone, his features hardened. Then, he would look at his dad, and they instantly softened to a loving, caring expression. Like his Grandma Roberts, he totally ignored the last rites that were in progress.

When the service ended, her old neighbors and friends began milling around, chatting and shaking hands before heading out. Rayden, without speaking a word to anyone, took one last look at the headstone, wheeled, and strode back to the funeral car in which he had ridden to the cemetery. He knew it would take his family back to the post-funeral luncheon. In his mind he also knew, he would *never* see that particular burial site again—*ever*.

Chapter 5

Mrs. Miller's death and funeral took up some of the extended time period while Jayden's family waited for the outcome of their commercial DNA tests. When the four reports were received via email on the same day, the similarities of the results were shocking to them. Jayden's showed 97% England, Wales, and Northwestern Europe and 3% Ireland and Scotland. The boy's tests were the same only 90% and 10% while Madelyn's showed 85% and 15%. The migration results to the new world were also similar.

That night at dinner, they held a family discussion.

"Dad," Ryan said. "Spend some money and have them do the full research on our DNAs. Maybe they'll show somebody out there who you're connected to other than us. If somebody else has taken the same test, it'll show up. A lot of my friends have learned about cousins they didn't even know existed."

"I don't know," Jayden said. "Do I want to find out if there's someone else out there I'm related to? Our lives are so good now; do we want to take a chance of stirring anything up? Besides, I could care less if I've got some kind of third cousin floating around out there someplace."

Rayden laid down his fork and glared at his dad. "Dad, we're not talking about a bunch of cousins and you know it. You've said right along you wanted to know who your real parents are. This *could* be your only chance. Don't blow it!"

"I don't know," Madelyn said. "I'm kind of with your dad on this. What if we all get our hopes up and there's nobody in the records? Or, what if somebody shows up who is, shall we say, not a real desirable type?"

Ryan looked at her. "Mom, that's not about to happen. I can't imagine someone who's *not a real desirable type* ever spending the extra money to carry the test further. It was expensive enough to do the first part."

"I want the full test done too," Rayden said—trying his best to look serious. "Maybe it'll tell me if Ryan is *really* my brother or nothing but a fake look-alike."

That broke any tension anyone felt, and everyone laughed. Only if they'd been identical twins, could anyone look more like his brother.

"I'm plenty comfortable with my parentage," Madelyn said. "So, I guess we don't have to do mine. Like your dad, I could care less learning about any distant cousins."

So, after some more discussion, the family made the decision together. Jay and the boys would have the expensive follow-ups done. That night, Jayden sat down at his computer with the boys looking over his shoulder as he finalized the application process and paid for the procedures.

After several weeks, the results of their tests once again returned via email. To no one's surprise, Jayden's confirmed the boys were his sons. But, then came the real shocker. The test results indicated a man, living in Florida, named William Ward Watson,Sr. was 95% sure to be Jayden's biological father. Below the man's name, the message also supplied a link where Jay could send the person a message.

As should be expected, the boys' results were identical. They showed each other as brothers and Jayden as their biological father. Their results also named the same person in Florida as their grandfather. The outcomes really stunned all of them.

• • •

Like every morning about seven am, William Watson, Sr. got up, made his bed, shaved, showered, and dressed. After taking his morning pills and pouring his first cup of coffee for the day, he sat down in front of his computer to check his bank accounts, credit cards, and investment funds before looking at his email. How many golden opportunities would he have that morning to balance his credit cards, remortgage his house, or buy something he *really, really* needed—like extended insurance on the car he'd sold three years previously? There were times he wondered why he even bothered. Ninety-five percent of the emails he received were pure garbage. However, that morning he received an email that would change his life forever.

A year previously, William and a group of his fellow professors and scientists who worked together at the university's robotics lab decided to take a commercial DNA test. For most of the group, it was done strictly for fun. Some of the people wanted to know where their ancestors came from, others hoped to find some long, lost relative, and others, like William, could care less. They did it because everyone else wanted to. Why not? What difference did it make to him if his heritage showed him to be the result of Norwegian marauders or southern European pirates?

The only relatives who meant anything to William were long gone. His parents had both died many years previously. He had lost his only child, a son, thirty-seven years before, and his wife the year after that. He had no other living relatives. He'd been an only child—as had both of his parents. There could be no cousins that he was aware of—other than maybe someone far-removed. The DNA test could give him nothing, but he still agreed to do it—just because.

As William scanned and deleted his emails, one towards the bottom caught his eye. It was from the genealogy company—first time he'd heard from them in ages. What on earth could they want? He'd already taken the full test. What were they trying to sell him this time? He almost deleted it without looking at it, but then opened it and read the thing. The message indicated new information about his family line which had recently been detected. It named a man in Michigan who was 95% sure to be his biological son. The test also indicated that there were two other people who were 90% certain to be his grandsons. He stared at the document. *No way! It couldn't be, could it?*

His mind flashed back thirty-seven years. His two-month old son had been abducted, and there had never been a trace of him seen, found, or heard of since. The authorities had worked tirelessly—especially one detective who never gave up. He'd kept the file on his desk until he retired. The abductor had been captured with the money in his pocket he'd been paid within an hour of the crime. How many times over the years had William wondered if his son were even still alive? As far as he knew, the case was still open at the police department. However, he didn't know for sure anymore. It's been a long time.

Holy crap! What am I going to do? DNA results are pure science. They don't lie. No way could this be a scam. Nowhere

in the application did I ever mention a child—much less
grandchildren. Does this mean little William is still alive?

William, Sr. looked at the email again. Below the
information, he saw a link he hadn't noticed before which
supposedly allowed him to contact the person named as his
biological son. No such links were given to his grandsons.
What was he going to do?

William took a deep breath, printed a copy of the
notification, slipped it into his pocket, and hustled out of his
condo. Twenty minutes later he walked into the robotics' lab at
the university. Amid all the greetings, several people waved at
him to join them. They had questions about projects they were
working on. He'd retired from his directorship position of the
lab six months previously and was still getting daily calls for
help. That morning he replied to their greetings, but told the
people with questions they had to wait. Before he could help
anyone else figure out their latest problem, he had to talk to the
new director, a brilliant scientist whom William had groomed
to replace himself.

The administrator was sitting in front of his computer when
William walked in. He stood and wrapped his arms around

William, hugging him warmly. "Will, am I ever glad to see you. This has been one of *those* days, and it has just started. I don't know why we ever let you out of this place? You're the only one who has a handle on everything we're trying to do around here."

William laughed, "Yeah, right! And, no, I'm not coming back here to work full time. Three days a week is bad enough—putting up with the cruel taskmaster who's running the show now."

"So, what are you up to, Will? This is your day off, you know. Or, am I assuming correctly that you just couldn't handle two days in a row without absorbing some of my charming personality?"

"Nope, I know, it's hard to believe, but that's not it," William said. "However, I do want to talk to you seriously for a minute or two. Unlike practically everyone else around here, you know I've never really cared or wanted to know all the gory details about my family's history. I took the DNA test because everyone else in the lab did. You and I have talked about it enough times, and we both know the only person in my family I've ever wondered about has been my son and whatever happened to him. So, I need you to read this and tell me what you think."

William took the paper out of his pocket and handed it to the director. Then he sat down in the guest chair in the office, watching and waiting.

"Oh my God, is this even possible? Could this person be your long-lost, kidnapped son?"

"I don't know," William said. "If it's true, he's alive and has two sons of his own—my grandsons."

"You emailed him, of course. What'd he have to say?"

"I haven't yet. That's why I wanted to come and talk to you. I just got the email this morning. I want to believe it, but I'm freaked out. I don't know what to do."

"Tell you what," the director said. "Go home and email this man right now and give him the historical basics, but not all the details. You might need them for confirmation purposes later. I don't know what that could be, but don't tell him everything. The main thing is to wait and see if he answers and what he has to say. If he does, and it sounds promising at all, the two of you can make arrangements to meet in a public place somewhere— either here or in Michigan. What the heck, Will, you haven't taken a vacation in a long time. Quit being such a miser and spend some of those millions you have stashed."

"Yeah, millions and millions, you got that right. I think it might better be referred to as the old and retired college-prof hoard."

"Seriously, Will, go home and send an email to the guy right now and see what happens—and for God's sake, keep me posted. If the other person is willing to meet up with you, you can fly up there and meet him—or he can fly down here. What can it hurt—except to open old wounds, but at least you would know for sure. It might even bring a little closure to thirty-some-odd years of pain. You won't know anything unless you try."

"Okay," William responded with a smile. "I'll go home and send him a note right now."

Also, Will, before you go, is it OK if I share the news with your friends here, or do you want to sit on it for now?

"Hey, everyone around here knows all my history. Go ahead and tell them. It'll give them something to talk about besides malfunctioning robots for the day. Also, tell all those people who had questions for me that I'll catch them tomorrow when I come in to work."

William slipped out the back door so he could avoid all the lab related inquiries. He had a job to do right then that was a lot more important.

Chapter 6

Gathered around the computer, Jayden's family talked. They needed a plan. Their preparation would be simple. Before they did any follow-up, Jayden and the boys would all get on their computers and do some research. They would use a combination of the man's name, home state, and email address to see what they could find out.

"Dad, look what I found," Ryan shouted. "That Mr. Watson dude is a *professor emeritus* at some university in Florida— whatever that means. He taught in the computer science department, and his specialty was robotic programming and software application development. Cool! I like the guy already."

Everyone gathered around behind Ryan, looking over his shoulders.

"Go to the university's archives and see if you can find any kind of a picture," Jayden said.

Ryan emailed the link to his dad and brother so they could bring up the site easily on their own computers and continue their searches.

After a short time, Ryan found a picture. It wasn't a great image, but one thing was clear. "Dad," Ryan screamed, "check this out. He kind of looks like you!"

"What? Let me see," Jayden said.

As the family gathered around Ryan's computer again, Madelyn shook her head. "Good Lord, how many more Jayden Miller look-alikes are there out there?"

"Um, yeah, Dad," Rayden said. "Any more of those look-alikes out there closer to our age we don't know about?"

"Behave yourself for once, would you?" Jayden laughed along with everyone else.

"So, what are we gonna do?" Rayden asked. "Let's send him a letter and see if he answers it."

"Alright, but I want all of us to think about this for a day before we do. What do you say that tomorrow night after dinner, the four of sit down together and compose a letter to this Mr. Watson?"

"Why do we have to wait until tomorrow?" Rayden asked. "Why don't we just do it right now?"

Jayden smiled. The boys had no idea how anxious the concept made him. "Several reasons, like how are we going to word it? How are we going to approach the subject? Will Mr. Watson have any idea what we are talking about? If he does, is he willing to even discuss it with strangers? Is he even aware that he had a son 37 years ago?"

"You mean like maybe he had some kind of one-night-stand with someone and has no idea you even exist?" Madelyn said.

"Exactly," Jayden said. "I didn't want to say it that way, but who knows? So, how much information are we willing to provide in the initial letter? We know nothing about him, and he knows nothing about any of us. That's what we need to think about before writing the letter."

Ryan leaned against his computer table with his chin in his hand. "What do you think, Dad? Would you be willing to meet up with the guy in a neutral site some place—that is, if he's also agreeable?"

"Why don't we all fly down to Florida and find the guy," Rayden said. "I want to meet him—now."

"No," his dad said. "If there's going to be a meet-up of any kind, it's going to be him and me the first time—alone. And, yes, Ry, I do like your idea. We can suggest that in the letter."

Way too soon for the boys, it was time for bed. However, the next day while their mothers and fathers were at work, the four teenaged cousins—Ryan, Rayden, and Rob's boys, Scott and Alex all hammered away on their computers looking for more and more information. From what they could find out, it looked as if Mr. Watson was either unmarried or widowed, retired, but still doing some part-time coordination in the computer science department of the university—much to the glee of Ryan, the family computer geek.

That night at dinner, the four boys shared with their own parents what they had found. Jay, Madelyn, and their boys spent the rest of their dinner rehashing potential points Jayden should or should not make in the initial letter. Of course, the biggest question in everyone's minds, would Professor Watson even respond? As the kids cleaned up the table and helped Madelyn with the dishes, Jayden sat down at the computer and opened up his private email account for the first time that day, he spotted a new message. The name on the email was William Ward Watson, Sr.

Before opening it, he shouted out to his wife and kids. "Hey, everyone, come down here. We've got to look at this together."

With Madelyn and the boys standing behind his chair, he opened the email. It read, "Thirty-eight years ago my two month old son, William Ward Watson, Jr., was abducted out of my wife's grocery cart at a local supermarket. We never saw him again. Today I received an email from the genealogy company where I had my DNA checked a year ago telling me there had been a recent match and the odds are 95% that you are that child. Would you please call me at the number I have provided below?"

Jayden turned around and made eye contact with his family.

Rayden wrapped his arm around his dad's neck and hugged him tightly. "Call him, Dad, *now*. If you want a little privacy, Ry and I will go upstairs. Just do it. You have to."

"Tell you what. Why don't you guys finish up the kitchen cleanup and then go jump in the pool? Mom and I need to talk. We can do that and keep an eye on you at the same time. Just make sure you stay in the shallow end until your hour after dinner is up."

The boys raced through their kitchen routine and then changed into their swimming suits in the pool's little changing room, a small, sealed off enclosure nestled between the fence and the edge of the pool. Both boys stood under the shower for maybe a whole five seconds or so, and then jumped into the shallow end of the pool. Instantly they started batting their water volleyball back and forth and the fun began.

Jay and Madelyn settled into the patio furniture. Madelyn slipped her hand over towards him, and he took hold of it. They sat quietly for a moment, watching the boys.

"You think I should call him?" Jay asked. "Suddenly, I find this whole situation extremely eerie. Is it a scam, some kind of a false reading, did somebody hack my account and try to set up a heist of some kind?"

"I think you're being paranoid. We now know that neither Mr. nor Mrs. Miller were your biological parents. Even in her demented stage, she has told you three different times that she bought you from somebody in Florida. A hacker would never know that. We also know from looking at the picture Ryan found, there is a strong family resemblance—speaking of something eerie. There's no reason why you can't fly south and meet him in a public restaurant the first time. Call him now while we're sitting here."

Chapter 7

After the genealogy company sent Jayden notification about a man in Florida who was 95% sure to be his biological father, he and his two sons initiated a massive Internet search, discovering as much information about the person as possible. A number of their findings looked positive. The family members talked it over and made a decision. The time had come. After Ryan and Rayden jumped into the pool, Jay and Madelyn sat on the patio, watching and talking. As the boys laughed and played two-man water volleyball, Jayden made the call.

He and Mr. Watson talked for close to an hour. The two of them created a plan. Jayden would fly to Orlando, Florida as soon as possible. Once there, he would rent a car and drive to the town where William lived. As soon as he settled into a motel, he would call Mr. Watson, and then the two would meet up for the first time at an agreed-upon restaurant to talk. In their hearts and minds, both men were hopeful, but cautiously skeptical. The whole scenario seemed too unbelievable to be true.

Jay left work early on Friday. When he got home, he threw his suitcase in the trunk, and then he, Madelyn, and the boys drove to a restaurant for a quick bite to eat. Afterwards, they took him to the airport and hugged and kissed him goodbye. After a changeover in Detroit, Jay flew non-stop to Orlando, picked up his rental, and drove an hour or so to the motel. After settling in, he called William Watson, Sr. again, and they made arrangements to meet the next day at a local restaurant for lunch at noon. Jayden had decided in advance he would not tell Mr. Watson what motel he was staying in, and William didn't ask.

The next day, Jayden sat at the back of the restaurant in a booth, checking his watch for the third time since he'd arrived. Then he looked up and saw the waiter escorting a gentleman towards him. Instantly, he stood and walked towards the man.

The first thing that flashed into Jay's mind was that the genetic physical similarities between him and his sons had to have originated at least one generation earlier. The man walking towards him carried the same height, physique, and facial expressions.

In disbelief of what they were seeing, the first words out of both of their mouths were, "Oh, my God!"

Both felt like they were looking in a mirror—one seeing an older version of himself, and the other looking at a younger edition. Smiling, they shook hands.

"Hello, Dad,"

"Hello, Son,"

After seeing each other in person, all of their questions regarding the validity of the DNA results vanished. After thirty-eight years, father and son had been reunited.

While eating lunch, Mr. Watson told Jayden the entire story of the abduction as he knew it. "Your birth name was William Ward Watson, Jr. When you were two months old, your mother took you to a supermarket one morning so she could buy groceries.

"Not able to find what she was looking for, she got distracted and left you lying in the cart while she wandered down an aisle looking for something. When she came back, you were gone. She screamed and fainted. The police were called. Security cameras had recorded the kidnapping with a full-face view of the culprit. Outside cameras showed the man walking to a car parked next to ours with you curled up in his left arm. He opened the passenger-side door and laid you in the front seat, without as much as a seatbelt or blanket, and drove off giving the cameras a full viewing of his license plate."

"Seems like that should have made it easy for the police to find the guy," Jayden said.

"It did. They spotted his vehicle and arrested the culprit in a little less than two hours. He had a record the length of your shirt sleeve—primarily as a drug addict who stole money for his heroin addiction. There were numerous warrants out for his arrest for theft, breaking and entering, and other petty crimes. He'd been caught on camera multiple times. When they arrested him and took him to the station, he told the police a wild story, claiming he had met a lady the day before in a park. He said when he spotted her, she was sitting on a bench crying.

He had intended to try to pan-handle a little money from her, but felt sorry enough to listen to her story, which she told willingly—everything but her name."

"So, that has to be the woman I grew up thinking was my mother," Jayden said.

"Apparently," Watson said," according to your abductor, she told him when they met the previous day, she had been fighting with her husband. According to her, they were unable to have children of their own, and her husband refused to adopt. She said he insisted he didn't want kids."

"This is so eerie. It's essentially the same story she told me in her demented state before she died. She'd gotten to the point where she made little sense most of the time, but this is basically her story too."

William shook his head and continued his side of the story. "Then she told the guy they intended to leave the next day around noon to go someplace out of state for his new job. Your kidnapper claimed she didn't tell him where. If she had, it might have made the initial search for you a little easier. Anyway, he said the lady insisted she wanted a baby, and didn't care how she got it."

73

Jayden frowned with a faraway look in his eyes. "Strange how some things never change. He *never* wanted me. He never liked me. So, how'd it happen?"

William continued, "The kidnapper said he made a deal with her. If she could come up $1,000 cash by the next day, he'd find her a baby."

Jayden shook his head at the craziness of the story. "He blew all their spare money on liquor. Where would she ever find a thousand dollars?"

"She said her husband had a stash hidden away for something-or-the-other in his suitcase and agreed to the deal. They would meet at ten the next morning at the same place in the park if he could find her a baby."

"So, how'd he ever think to look for me at a grocery store, of all places?" Jayden asked.

"Apparently, the super market had been, for all-intents-and-purposes, an accident. After they separated at the park, he spent the rest of the day trying to find a baby to steal with no success. Being a single man in his twenties, it never dawned on him that children are left unattended all the time in stores as their caregivers get distracted and wander all over the place without them.

"The next morning, he drove to the local supermarket, intending to do a little panhandling, and then hopefully pick up some beer. He claimed he'd given up on finding a baby by then. After parking, he was smoking a cigarette before going into the store when another vehicle pulled up beside him. It was my wife and your mother, Caroline. She got out of her car and walked around to the passenger side, opened up the back door, and took you out of your seat. He watched as the two of you went into the store."

Jayden sat there open mouthed, finding the story mind-blowing. "After he'd given up on stealing a baby—Bam! The two of us showed up."

"That's pretty much how it happened," William said. "He watched until the two of you got into the store, and then slinked around, following you while waiting to see what might happen. Sure enough, when Caroline wandered down an aisle and left you unattended, the kidnapper scooped you out of the cart and ran."

"And, just like that, I became a victim of human trafficking," Jayden said.

"Exactly. Within the next hour, the thief had his $1,000, and the lady, who I now realize was Mrs. Miller, had herself a new baby. I guess that's when you, William Ward Watson, Jr., became Jayden Scott Miller. Just think, within two hours of your abduction thirty-eight years ago, your kidnapper was arrested with the money still in his pocket, but you've been out of my life ever since—until today."

"All of that happened within a period of just a couple of hours, and nobody ever spotted me? Seems like it had to have been in the news," Jayden said.

William, looking forlorn, continued to speak. "Oh, believe me, it was on every television station in the state, but the police and FBI had zero luck finding you and your new mother. Unfortunately, back in those days, the park where the transition took place didn't have cameras like it does today. A photo shot of her face surely would have helped in her identification and possible capture and arrest. Someone would have recognized her. If nothing else, I guess we were lucky the grocery store had video security. At least they were able to catch and convict the original culprit. No idea if he's still in jail or not. Really don't care. With everything I had to go through, I flushed him out of my mind forever."

"Yeah, cameras at the park might've helped," Jayden said. "But who really knows, since the three of us left the state that afternoon. Even if someone had recognized her, we'd have been gone. Anyway, whatever happened to Caroline, my mother?"

"After you were gone without a trace, she sank into a dark depression. She blamed herself. She never should have left you unattended. Times were different then, and we didn't understand the seriousness of her despair. If we had, we would have found her help. Anyway, one year to the day after you were kidnapped, according to the credit card data, she filled the gas tank in her automobile with gasoline at nine in the morning, drove to the supermarket where you were stolen, and parked the car in the same general location she had been a year previously." William paused and looked off into space.

After a moment, Jayden asked, "What did she do then?"

"She got out of the car and attached a vacuum cleaner hose to the exhaust pipe and then fed it through the back window.

All the other windows were closed tightly. The window with the hose was open just enough to hold it in place. Later that afternoon, when I got home from work, she was nowhere around, and I couldn't get a hold of her. I checked with some of her friends, and nobody had seen or heard from her all day. I called 911 and reported her missing. That evening the police found her body, locked in the car with the engine still running."

"And nobody in the parking lot ever saw what was happening and called the authorities?"

"Hard to believe, isn't it?" William said. "How could people be so oblivious or uncaring, they could walk by and not notice something like that happening or totally ignore it if they did?"

When William paused again, Jay looked at him and spoke, "Did you ever remarry?"

"No. I've never even dated anyone during the thirty-seven years since Caroline passed. My whole life—social and work, has revolved around my job. I became the department head in the computer-science division of the university until I retired last year. During my later years, I specialized in robotics— which included both programming and application development. I loved it, but when the university made a lucrative retirement offer to us old-timers, it was something I couldn't refuse. Since then, I've been helping them out a little on a part time basis three days a week, but the rest of the time I sit around the house with nothing to do but watch television as I drive myself batty. Jay, I hate that way of life, and the sad part is, I had no idea that things could or would ever get better."

Jay smiled with a faraway look in his eyes. "Ironic point for the day? My adoptive Mom Roberts has never dated either in the past 37-38 years. She was widowed when a tank blew up in Iraq. She too has always been too busy and preoccupied—working, taking care of kids, and in general not interested.

Chapter 8

After hearing the story of his own abduction and mother's suicide, Jay shared the story of his abusive childhood at the hands of the lady who had bought him and her evil husband. Then he told William about his wife and two sons. He also told his dad about his discombobulated adoptive/step family of Mom Roberts, his brother Rob and his wife and his two nephews, Scott and Alex, who were the same ages as his own sons.

After leaving the restaurant, Jayden and his dad went to William's condo and spent the rest of the day updating each other on their pasts. At one point when they were laughing and talking about the genetic similarities of their own appearance—size, build, facial shapes, expressions and smiles, Jayden pulled out his cell phone. "You haven't seen the best part yet. Look at these three pictures."

William looked at the pictures of Jayden at fourteen and his two boys—who were currently fifteen and fourteen. He smiled and dug out his own phone, showing Jayden a picture of himself at the ripe-old-age of 14 as well. It had been an old school picture which one day, just for the fun of it, he'd photocopied to his phone.

Jayden took one look and laughed. "This is unbelievable. Text it to me. I've got an idea."

William did, so Jayden could put the four pictures together in a folder on his phone of the boys, himself, and the image of Mr. Watson.

Looking at it was a lot of fun and kind of mind-blowing. William spoke first. "Sometimes genetics are crazy. If you ignore the dated clothing and focus on our faces, you'd think we were looking at quads. Want to know what's even weirder? My father and I looked just alike as well."

Jayden looked at his dad and grinned, "Really? It's a four-generation genetic boondoggle. We all look alike. That's crazy!"

William laughed. "I wonder what the boys will think of this."

"That's why I wanted you to send it to me. You want to have some fun?"

"Sure. What do you have in mind?"

"I'll make a new folder with these four pictures and crop them so they only show everyone from the neck up. Then I'll send the thing to the boys and see if they can pick you out of the crowd."

"Sounds like fun. Let's do it."

It only took a couple of minutes, and the new compilation was complete.

William laughed, "If I hadn't watched you do it, I'm not sure I could pick myself out of the crowd. Do you ever mix the boys up, or aren't they really all that close in the flesh?"

"Oh yeah, all the time when one walks into the room by himself and not talking, a lot of times Maddie and I both have to do a double-take. But, when they're standing next to each other, it's no huge problem. Ryan is almost an inch taller and maybe ten pounds heavier. Also, his voice has dropped a little lower than Ray's so that always helps. When you get to know them, you'll pick up on the little subtleties."

"I want to meet them."

"I think that's gonna happen—real soon."

While they talked, Jayden made a special background design around the folder. When he finished, he labeled the images A, B, C, and D—Ryan, Grandpa, Rayden, and Jayden. Then he sent the collection to the three at home along with a message. "OK, boys, your allowance is at stake. One of these four pictures is a shot of your Grandpa Watson when he was fourteen. Your job for the day is to decide which one is your grandpa and send me your answer. If you don't choose the correct image, I get to spend your next week's stipend."

Within seconds, his screen lit up.

"Dad, not fair. All four of those pictures are of us," Rayden said.

"Tell the truth, Dad. Is one of them really Grandpa? I don't believe it," Ryan said.

Madelyn was a little more subtle, "Dirty pool. Since *my* allowance isn't in jeopardy, I pick A."

After more whining, the boys made their selections known. Ryan chose C and Rayden D. Nobody picked B.

After all the votes were in, Jayden sent Grandpa's eighth grade school picture complete with dated clothing along with another message, "*NOW* I have to decide what I'm going to spend *all* my extra money on next week."

Much to the delight of Jayden and Grandpa Watson, a chorus of groans, whines, and boos followed.

Chapter 9

That night Mr. Watson had trouble sleeping. Flipping and flopping, his mind churned continuously. Finally, he got out of bed and cranked up his computer, and instigated several Google searches. The next morning at breakfast, he didn't know if he wanted to mention what he had discovered or not.

"Dad, is something wrong?" Jayden said. "You're looking troubled. You're not having second thoughts or anything, are you?"

"No, no, nothing like that. I couldn't get the story out of my head that you told me yesterday at lunch about the *original* Jayden dying of SIDS. Since I couldn't sleep, I spent some time last night doing some research. I think I found the cemetery where the original Jayden Scott Miller is buried. You interested at all in visiting it?"

"Wow! Never even thought about looking for him, and yes, I would. However, there is something about the whole scenario that strikes me as somewhat amusing. It has to be my weird sense of humor getting to me again."

"What's that?" William asked. His fear that maybe he had delved in forbidden territory had vanished.

Jayden looked at his dad and smiled before speaking. "My sons discovered and showed Madelyn and me the burial plot of the man we all *thought* was my father. And now, my *real* father has discovered the burial plot of the original me. Let's go this morning when we leave here and see if we can find it."

The two finished breakfast at the neighborhood restaurant, chatting non-stop, bouncing from one topic to another. They had thirty-eight years to catch up on.

As Jayden paid the bill, he looked over at William. "I would like to visit my mother's grave as well. Can we do that first?"

"Sure," William said. "The two cemeteries are actually pretty close to each other. We can visit Caroline's on the way to Jayden's."

"Is there a florist we can stop into nearby? I'd like to buy a dozen roses."

"Sure," William said, smiling at his son—thinking to himself what might have been.

Mr. Watson had done a good job of maintaining Caroline's grave over the years. A flower-filled urn sat between her and what would someday be William's grave. In front of the stone sat two white geraniums and a pink Wave Petunia.

"It's beautiful," Jayden said as he stood in front of the stone, admiring the scene.

"I usually come out here three or four times a year—and, always just before Memorial Day to decorate and then again around Labor Day. I try to keep it looking nice."

William stooped down and pulled a couple of weeds as they continued to talk. After fifteen minutes or so, they walked back to William's car and left.

"Wow!" Jayden said as they drove down the cemetery road to the street leading to the other cemetery. "That was my mother, a mother I never knew even existed until now, yet I feel moved by our visit." He looked over at William, "Dad, I *will* visit her again—hopefully, at least once a year."

Not a whole lot more was said as the two men drove, deep in thought, to the cemetery listed on Jayden Scott Miller's obituary. When they arrived, they checked in at the office. The receptionist quickly looked up the location and gave them directions.

Father and son stood shoulder to shoulder and stared at the dirty, diminutive, and uncared for stone and grave site. Grass nearly covered the site. The cemetery maintenance men had not trimmed too closely around the stone as they did with well-cared for plots.

Jayden pulled out his cell phone and took a picture. He looked over at his dad. "I am betting in the thirty-eight years the little guy has lain here, he's never had a flower planted for him."

"I have a trowel and three-pronged hand hoe which I use on Caroline's plot stashed at home in my apartment. Let's do it," William said.

Two hours later, the men once again stood over the grave. They cleared the stone of grass on all four sides, and then washed, and polished it. Soon two red geraniums and a purple wave petunia adorned the site. Jayden took another picture.

He looked over at his dad. "I think I'm getting weird in my old age."

William laughed. "Why? What makes you say that?"

"For some reason, I feel a strange attachment to the original Jayden—like, he's a long lost brother or something from my childhood."

"I don't find that strange at all," William said. "From what you've told me about your brother Rob, your Mom, and nephews, why should this be any different? You're the one who used the word, 'discombobulated' when describing your family. This fits the mix perfectly—that is, providing you include me. A day ago you met your dad, this morning you've met the burial place of another mom and another brother. Personally, I can't wait to meet the rest of the live members of the clan."

Sunday afternoon the two of them boarded a plane together. Mr. Watson would be flying with Jayden to Michigan for a couple of weeks to meet *his* new family. They decided in advance not to purchase round-trip tickets for William. They'd make a decision about his return to Florida later. The estimated two-week timetable they originally decided on would be flexible. They both wanted to see how things went after William and the rest of the family had a chance to get together and meet.

Chapter 10

Jayden and William walked side-by-side down the steps at the airport.

"My God, Jay, they're identical," William said when he spotted the boys waiting below with Madelyn.

"Almost, but not quite," Jayden said. "If you look closely, Ryan, the older one of the two is on our right. He's just a touch taller and a few pounds heavier."

When they walked up to Madelyn and the boys, Grandpa Watson hugged Madelyn, and then looked over at the boys. He stuck out his hand and said, "Hello, Ryan. Great to meet you."

Then he turned to Rayden and grabbed his hand. "Hi, Ray, very happy to meet you, too."

"How'd you know which one of us was which?" Ryan asked.

"Dad ratted us out," Rayden said. "Didn't you see them talking and Dad pointing at us on their way down the steps? You know he doesn't play fair."

All of them laughed as they headed for the luggage carousel.

When they got home, Grandpa unpacked and settled into the guest room. Afterwards, the family headed out to the patio. As the boys swam, the adults talked.

While they conversed, William kept an eye on the boys in the water. "Except for cannonballs, I haven't seen either boy do an actual dive. Don't they do that?"

Jayden shook his head, "No, not really. Probably 'cause nobody around here has ever taken it seriously. Both boys are good swimmers, but neither one has shown any interest in actual diving or the school's swimming team. They just like to play and have fun. Let's face it, for them, the pool is nothing but a big toy. Most of their time is taken up with academics and their hobbies—you know, like I mentioned, Ryan's robots and Rayden's chemistry. Thank goodness, neither one has had a serious accident yet with their experiments."

Grandpa kept watching the boys with interest. "Wonder if either would be interested in learning to dive. I was on both my high school and university swim teams. I actually won some awards for diving."

"Really?" Madelyn said. "Part of the problem is, nobody around here has ever been knowledgeable enough about diving to teach them how. I'll bet if you asked them, they'd at least be willing to try—especially some of those tricky dives swim teams perform."

"Maybe I'll do that," Grandpa said. "Not today, but sometime in the next day or so I'll get into the water with the boys and show them a couple of flips. If they decide they want to try some, I'll show them how it's done."

The next day, Grandma Roberts, Rob, and his gang showed up. After introductions all around and decisions made as to all of their relationships, they once again worked their way out to the pool. Since Jayden and Rob were "adoptive" or "step" brothers, for simplicity sake, Grandpa became Rob's step-dad and his boys' step-grandpa. Of course, nobody bothered with the "step" word unless trying to explain the relationship to friends.

As always, Rob's boys brought their suits with them, so shortly after arriving all four boys were in the pool. While doing that, Jay and Rob warmed up the grill and started the 'hangleburgers.' They had never let Rayden live down some of his early child hood pronunciations. The three ladies went into the house to get the rest of the meal ready while Grandpa Watson watched the boys from his chair.

Jay noticed what was going on and walked over to his dad. "You want to borrow one of my suits? Might be a trifle tight, but I think I've got one you could get into it."

William did, so the two of them went in and checked on Jay's spare suits. One had an elastic band, making it a bit more stretchable so he decided to try that one. Ten minutes later, Grandpa walked out to the pool and headed straight to the board. He walked down to the end of it, bounced up and down a couple of times, and then walked back to the starting point. He loped down the board, bounded high, and did a double flip before landing perfectly.

When the four boys saw Grandpa headed for the board, all stopped what they were doing and watched with their mouths wide open.

"How did you do that?" Scott yelled from the shallow end.

"C'mere, and I'll show you," Grandpa said.

An hour later, all four boys were doing an acceptable single flip and landing without making a small tidal wave.

Sunday night, before the boys went to bed, Madelyn dug into her purse and handed them their allowance for the coming week. The boys looked at each other, knowing what was on the other one's mind. Without speaking, they walked over to where their dad sat on the sofa, talking to Grandpa Watson and held out their hands—which had firm grips on their money.

Jayden looked at his two sons and smiled. He'd forgotten the stunt he'd pulled on them with the pictures. "Ten percent goes in your savings account, and the rest is yours. You know darned well I was joking."

Ryan smiled in relief. "Thanks, Dad. But, we had to make sure."

Rayden had the same expression. "Thanks, Dad. Maybe this week I'll even put in twenty percent just because. Besides,

I've still got some of last week's that I didn't spend 'cause I figured I'd have to make it stretch into two weeks."

Jayden stood and pulled both of his kids into a hug and said, "Enjoy and spend it wisely. Time for bed, boys."

The next day when Jay and Madelyn went to work, the boys asked if it would be OK if Grandpa watched them in the swimming pool. The family rules indicated no swimming or playing in the pool without an adult present. In the past, that had always meant Jay, Rob, Rob's wife, Madelyn, or Grandma. Naturally, Mom and Dad agreed as long as Grandpa was OK with it. The boys, however, were *not* to take advantage of him. After all, he had things to do on his schedule—like checking out the computer science labs at the university where Jayden worked.

By ten o'clock, Scott and Alex arrived at the Millers' house with their swim suits. Grandpa and the four boys were still in the pool when Jay and Madelyn came home from work. Fortunately, they had taken a break for lunch. Grandpa felt and looked exhausted. The four boys showered away the chlorine and changed back into their street clothes. Rob's boys headed home to dinner while Grandpa showered, dressed, and plopped into a chair.

After dinner, the family settled into their spots in the living room to watch the news and talk about their days. Grandpa looked over at Jayden. "I think Scott really gets into this diving thing. He's always the first to perfect whatever dive we're working on and then wants to try something new. When the other three had enough and wanted to play water volleyball, he kept going."

After the chatter settled down to just an occasional comment, everyone started reading or watching the Tiger game with the sound turned low. After a bit, Ryan looked over at his grandpa. "Would you mind coming downstairs with me and looking at something?"

"Ryan, Grandpa's tired. Can't it wait until tomorrow?" Jayden said.

"Hey, it's OK. We're good," Grandpa said, curious as to what Ry had in mind. He set down his Kindle, stood, and followed his grandson down the steps.

After fifteen minutes or so had passed, Jayden looked over at Rayden. "Take a peek down the steps and see what those two are up to. Don't bother them; just see if you can figure out what they're doing. I'm betting it has something to do with Ryan's robot that doesn't always want to work exactly the way he thinks it should—even though everybody else thinks it's working fine."

A couple of moments later, with a gigantic smile on his face, Ray slipped back into the living room. "You should see them. They're both on their hands and knees, heads down and butts up," he said jabbing his thumb upwards. "Ryan's going after his creepy robot with a screwdriver and Grandpa's pointing at something. Who knows what?"

A short time later, the two popped back into the living room. "It works!" Ryan shouted happily. "Grandpa fixed it."

"I didn't fix it. You did," Grandpa said.

"I just did what you told me to do."

Madelyn laughed. "I guess it doesn't matter who did what. The main thing is it finally works to your satisfaction, and you're obviously happy about it."

"You're never that happy when one of my experiments works. Why not?" Rayden asked his mom, pretending to be offended.

"I'm just happy when you finish whatever you're doing and the house is still in one piece," Madelyn said.

Grandpa looked over at Rayden. "You know, chemistry was my minor in college. If you ever have any questions about one of your experiments, let me know. Maybe I can help."

"Tomorrow morning before we go out and start jumping off the diving board, I want you to show me something. I've got a problem that's been driving me nuts, and *nobody* around here knows *anything* about chemistry. It's physics, robotics, and medicine. Nobody but me is interested in the good stuff."

Chapter 11

On Saturday morning, at the end of Mr. Watson's first week in Michigan, he decided he wanted to visit the cemetery where the Millers were buried. Jayden had told him about the place and Rayden's issues with it, so, for some reason or the other, Grandpa wanted to see it and didn't really know why. Was it morbid curiosity? Was it elation because the people who'd kidnapped his son were dead and gone? He had no idea. The only thing he knew for sure was, the bodies lying in those graves were the people who'd bought his baby from a kidnapper thirty-eight years earlier and destroyed his marriage and life. Not only that, but those same people had abused his son horribly and never loved nor wanted him.

As Mom, Dad, and Grandpa were getting around and ready to go, Ryan and Rayden were shooting baskets in the driveway.

Madelyn called for them to come into the house. When they walked into the living room, she told them, "We're going to take a ride over to the cemetery to show Grandpa Mr. and Mrs. Miller's grave sites. Besides, I'm sure the flowers need watering. When we leave, we're going to get a bite to eat."

"*I'm not going*," Rayden snarled. "I'm staying here."

"But, Honey, we're going out to eat at you and your dad's favorite restaurant."

"Go without me. I'm *never* gonna go to that place again unless you and Dad *make* me. Don't worry about me, Mom. I'll put together a couple of peanut butter and jelly sandwiches."

"OK, OK, calm down. We'll stop back by the house and pick you up when we're on our way to the restaurant."

"You don't *have* to."

"We will," Madelyn told him with raised eyebrows. "Now, listen to me—carefully. While we're gone, you go back outdoors and shoot layups. And, I want you to do them the way I tell you. Run as fast as you can at least twenty feet for each shot, dribbling first right handed and the next time with your left. Do that for every layup and burn off a little of that attitude."

"Mom, I'm sorry."

"We won't be gone long, Honey, so don't work up too big a sweat. We don't want you stinking up the restaurant."

She pulled him to her, gave him a quick hug, and then kissed his cheek.

As the rest of them backed out of the driveway, Grandpa looked out the window at Rayden who by then was alone in the backyard, about twenty feet from the end of the garage, dribbling hard with his right hand and glaring up at the basket. "Boy, he's upset. Wonder why going to the cemetery set him off so badly."

"Because he's a classic daddy's boy," Ryan said as a matter of fact.

"Ryan," Jayden said. "That's not nice."

"Hey! Mom and Grandma call him that all the time. You know darned well he can't stand those people for what they did to you. And now, after we've heard the latest news about the kidnapping and all that, it makes his resentment and anger all the worse."

Madelyn smiled. She wanted to break a little of the tension if she could. "When did you ever hear Grandma or me call him a daddy's boy?"

"I've got ears."

"You've got horns," she said smiling.

With the topic of conversation suddenly switched to Ryan and his *listening in* on his mom and grandma's conversations, the atmosphere in the car lightened big time.

After a quick visit to the cemetery, the family swung back by the house and picked up Rayden. He sat quietly for the ride to the restaurant while the others chatted about everything and anything other than the cemetery.

When they got to their table, Ray grabbed the seat next to Jayden. He looked at him and asked, "Dad, are you OK?"

Jay looked at him seriously, "Yes, I am. How about you?"

"Not really. Like I told Mom, I'll never go to that place again unless you make me. Not only that, I really don't want to know about it if and when you go either."

Jay reached over, and hugged Rayden to him, who melted into his dad's right side.

"Ray, I'm good with that."

Chapter 12

After some research and numerous chats with Madelyn, Jayden called his dad. Just before it went to voice mail, his father answered the phone.

"Hey, what's up this fine, sunny Friday morning? Didn't think for a minute you were going to answer," Jayden said.

"Oh, I didn't have the phone with me. Alex was the closest and raced up to the patio to grab it for me. Scott and I have an important project going—double flips off the diving board without leaving a ripple."

"Oh, good grief! Do those kids give you any peace at all?"

"You know I love it. Scott wanted to practice his diving, and the others wanted to swim and play water volleyball. It's a lot more fun for me to hang with them than to stare mindlessly at the TV back in Florida," Grandpa said.

"Any chance you can break away from that mob around noon so you and I can take a little side trip? The four of them are NOT invited. Want to show you something in private," Jayden said.

"Sure. I'll be ready. Gonna give me a heads up?"

"Nope. See you at 12:20. I'll leave the university at noon."

When Jayden pulled into the driveway, all four boys stood on the driver's side waiting to attack while their grandpa climbed into the passenger's seat and snapped the seatbelt around him.

"Why can't we go?" Rayden said. "You know there aren't supposed to be any big secrets around here anymore."

"That's not what Santa told me."

"*Dad*!"

The other five in the group all laughed at Ray's expense as Jay backed out of the drive.

"So, where are we going, if I may be so bold to ask?" Grandpa said, still laughing at Ray's reaction.

"About two blocks from here. Won't take us but a couple of minutes to get there."

"You know, when we're done, I'd like to have a serious discussion with you. I've got something weighing on my mind," Watson said.

"Sure, when we're through, let's go grab a sandwich and cup of coffee. We can talk there," Jayden said.

Jay pulled into one of the guest parking spaces in front of a large brick building which his dad had not seen during his two week visit. When they got out of the car, a gentleman dressed in a suit coat and tie greeted them.

"Dad, I want you to meet the building's real estate agent, Tom Johnson. Tom, this is my dad, William Watson."

The two shook hands with greetings, and then the three of them walked into the building.

After introductions were also made to the building manager, they stopped at the elevator. When they walked into the open door, William still had no clue what was going on except that it was obvious the meeting had been prearranged. The elevator came to a halt on the sixth floor and the group stepped out. They walked down about three doors and paused. Tom punched a security code into the lock, and the door opened.

He stood aside allowing Jay and William to enter ahead of him. Leaving the door open, he followed them. Then he spoke, "This condo was owned last by an elderly couple. When the man passed, the woman moved to the west side of the state to be with her kids. The place has been offered at a reasonable price. Considering it comes completely furnished, it's downright cheap. She had no use for any of the furniture, so about all she took were her personal items. The way it works out, after paying the base rate for the condo, the furnishings are free."

They continued to walk around the place while the real estate agent showed them all the amenities—which included a view overlooking a small wooded area and pond. Then he showed William the owner's private parking space right outside the door on the sixth floor ramp. Guest parking was in front of the building.

"Wow! This place is impressive. I love what I see. How expensive is it?" William said.

"Let's sit down at the dining room table, and I can go over everything with you—including building fees, utilities, taxes, etc." Tom said.

When the agent finished, William told him, "On the surface, I'm blown away. But, I can't decide one way or the other right this minute. I need to talk to Jay and everyone else in the family first."

When the two of them left and reached the parking lot, William looked at Jay as he snapped his seat belt. "You've been reading my mind."

"Why?" Jayden said smiling, "Is this what you wanted to talk about when we left the house?"

"Yes, how did you know?"

"Don't you think that maybe all of us have been thinking the same thing? Your whole family lives here. I don't want to pressure you, but I think this is where you belong too. Madelyn and I have even discussed a potential financial plan where we could pay for the condo up front to make it happen immediately if it would help. What say we forget about you heading back to Florida right away and take some time to make a rational decision?

Besides, Ryan and Scott need more practice time behind the wheel. From what I'm hearing, it seems like you're the *only one* who's been willing to go driving with them lately."

"God, they're good kids. Love 'um all to pieces. Let's go grab that bite to eat and talk."

Two hours later they left the restaurant, filled with warm, glazed, cream cheese muffins, coffee, and a plan. Jay would clue in Madelyn, his mom, and Rob on the arrangement, and then after the family cookout on the patio Saturday afternoon, they would tell the four boys and see what kind of feedback they might have to offer.

When Jay and William got home, all the boys were kicking a soccer ball around the backyard and full of questions. As could be expected, they got no answers. Adults could be *so* irritating at times.

As the family sat around the patio Saturday afternoon, after eating and chatting about everything and anything on their minds, nothing had been mentioned yet about Grandpa possibly staying permanently.

As the conversations were beginning to wane, Grandpa looked over at Rayden. "Ray, you've been scowling at me ever since we ate. What gives? Am I in trouble?"

Numerous grins and chuckles appeared as all the others contemplated Grandpa being in trouble with Rayden.

"We need to talk."

"I'm all ears," Grandpa said. "Is this going to be a public or private conversation?"

"Public," Rayden said, still frowning slightly.

"OK, what's going on?"

"The four of us have been talking about something—that is, me, Ry, Scott, and Alex. We've decided you can't go back to Florida. You've gotta stay here. This is where you belong. Grandpa, we *need* you."

"But, I've lived in Florida my entire life. I have a home there. You think I should just throw all of those connections away and stay here?"

"Yes. I guess the main and most important thing is, you're retired, and we're your family. And, we're all here. There's no reason why you can't stay here. Besides that, there are a bunch of other reasons why you should," Rayden said.

The rest of the family sat back, still smiling and listening, while looking back and forth between Rayden and Grandpa who, by that time, had totally focused on each other.

"So, clue me in," Grandpa said. "What are all of those *other* reasons?"

Rayden leaned forward and stared directly into his grandpa's eyes. "*My* dad and Uncle Rob have never known what it was like to have a *real* father like the four of us have. Uncle Rob never had anyone period. His dad died in the Iraqi war when Uncle Rob was a baby. My dad had a piece of crap who didn't even want him, abused him, and made life miserable for him. Since you've been here, both of our dads have had a father they could talk to, relate to, and love—a father who actually cared for and about them. All of that is plenty of reason enough, but there's still a lot more."

"And, I'm *still* listening."

Rayden continued, stone faced. "We think the four of us kids are important too. Look what you've done in just a little over two week's time. For starters, you've taught us how to dive instead of just cannon-balling off the board. Scott is getting really, really good at it. He loves it. He wants to try out for the school's swim team next year—something none of us have ever even considered. He knows he *needs* more lessons, and you're the one to give them to him.

"Ryan and Scott have both accumulated, who knows, how many hours behind the wheel driving with you teaching and helping them. You've probably taken them out seven or eight times in just the couple of weeks you've been here. When they hit their sixteenth birthdays, they want to be ready to pass their drivers' tests and get their licenses. You can help make that happen. And, next year, it'll be Alex's and my turns.

"And look what else you've done for Ryan. You've given him a ton of help with that robot thing of his He says he can't even begin to thank you enough. He had no clue what he'd done to screw it up, and nobody else around here knew enough of that kind of programming to help. He thought he would have to wait until school started up again in September before he could get it going the way he wanted it. Now, I think he knows more about it than the robot does about itself. You have no idea how much more peaceful it is around here when his stupid "toy" isn't outsmarting him.

"And, you've been tutoring Alex in all those high-tech math computations he loves to mess around with continuously. The only other person around here who even knows what he's doing is Dad, and he works all the time, so you've been a lifesaver there as well.

"And look what you've done for me. Every time I have a question on one of my chemistry experiments, you've been right here explaining things to me so they actually make sense. I'm not just guessing or taking a stab in the dark anymore."

Red-faced, Rayden stopped for a couple of seconds—long enough for Grandpa to interrupt.

"You're giving me an awful lot of credit for doing what any normal person would do in my position."

"That's just the point," Rayden said. "We didn't have a *normal* person in your position who was willing and able to do the things you've done for us. We love you, and we love having you in our lives. Don't leave!"

Grandpa looked over at his other grandsons, who had all been sitting there stone-faced without speaking during Rayden's spiel. "What about the rest of you? You agree with what Ray's been saying?"

Ryan spoke first as the others nodded their heads in agreement. "Very definitely, all four of us agree on this. We picked Ray to tell you what we think and wanted you to know because he's the one of us who *should* become a lawyer like Uncle Rob, instead of some kind of crazy chemist who's apt to burn down the house or fumigate us all in our sleep some night when he screws something up."

Grandpa laughed before speaking. "You know, you might have a great idea with that lawyer conclusion. There's a need out there for attorneys who specialize in things like getting patents for scientists and others who actually know something about what they are dealing with. If I were trying to get a patent for a project I was working on, I'd definitely want a representative who knew as much about the field as possible. And, let's face it. Ray is pretty darned good about getting his point across."

That comment brought a few more chuckles from the adults of the group who had been sitting back listening and not entering into the conversation.

Rayden took a deep breath and then exhaled a little noisier than normal. "So, Grandpa, are you going to stay here with us or not?"

"Well, your dad did take me to check out an awfully nice-looking condominium yesterday that's only a couple of blocks from here. It's even furnished a lot nicer than the old stuff I've been living with for years. You know, I'd planned on going back to Florida next week, but I've cancelled those plans. I guess it's a good thing I didn't get a round trip ticket after all."

"I want to see the condo," Ryan said. "Will you show it to us tomorrow?"

"Well, I can show you the outside—providing you or Scott is willing to drive us over to the place. More than likely, we can't go inside without the real estate agent, and tomorrow will be a Sunday, so I doubt if he'd be available."

"Unless, of course, the building manager is around and willing to let us in," Jayden said, speaking for the first time since the discussion had started. "I'll give him a call. He should remember us from yesterday."

The rest of the day was spent discussing what would have to be done to get Grandpa moved. They created a tentative plan. After the condo purchase was completed, and he had taken possession, he would fly back to Florida, taking Rayden and Alex with him to gather up and pack his personal belongings, clothing, and anything else he wanted to bring with him. The boys' job would be to do all of the manual work of hauling, lifting, packing, and stacking.

Jay, Rob, Ryan, and Scott would drive—giving the boys two-hour shifts behind the wheel. Most of their practice had been city driving. This would give the two of them plenty of highway experience traveling back and forth.

The furniture items Grandpa didn't want to keep could be donated to either Good Will or Volunteers of America. Anything they didn't want would be left in the residence or thrown away. Years before retiring from teaching at the university, William had sold his house and downsized to an apartment. Since his original lease had run out, he remained living there on what was referred to as a month-to-month basis. Therefore, turning his apartment back over to the company would be fast and effortless. Building management would have to be notified, and they would take care of refurbishing and releasing the place.

The only question left was where would the boys sleep while they were there? His apartment only had one-bedroom.

Grandpa thought he had the answer for that one. "No biggie, the boys can share the bed, and I'll sleep on the couch."

"No way," barked Rayden. "Alex can sleep on the couch. He's a couple of months older than I am and a lot more spoiled. I'll sleep on the floor. That's no big deal. All I need is a pillow and a blanket to keep me warm. If you don't have carpet, I can roll up in the blanket and still be plenty comfortable."

"Well, my couch does pull out into one of those sofa beds. I've never opened it up, but we should be able to figure it out."

"Problem solved," Alex said. "Ray and I share the sofa, and you keep your bed. I get the inside so in case he starts snoring too loud, I can push him off onto the floor."

"I don't snore!" Rayden scowled.

Everyone but Rayden laughed. After looking around at the rest of the family, he did smile, realizing he'd been set up— again.

That night, after Uncle Rob and his family had gone home, and the boys were about ready to hit the showers and bed, Rayden couldn't help himself from being Rayden. "You know, Grandpa, living in a condo will mean you're going to miss out on one of the greatest pleasures of living in Michigan. You won't have any snow to shovel. So, any time it snows and you feel like you're being cheated, you can always come over here and give Ryan and me a hand. We have two shovels, so we can all take turns passing them back and forth between us. We'll *gladly* share."

Grandpa Watson rolled his eyes and shook his head. "Aren't you supposed to be going to bed?"

Again, everyone laughed.

Jayden couldn't help but getting into the conversation. "You know, Dad, traveling through all that snow around here isn't really all that bad for us. Before we get plowed out, we always hook Rayden up to a dogsled and make him pull us wherever we need to go."

Rayden fought to hold back his smirk while everyone else snorted at his expense. Then, with a straight face, he glared at his dad. "*Junior, behave yourself.*"

Everyone held their breath for a second to see what Jayden's reaction might be.

"Didn't Grandpa say something about you two belonging in bed? Go."

They did, with both of them snickering on their way up the steps. It was the first time anyone in the family had referred to Jayden as William, Jr.

When the boys closed their bedroom door, Jayden looked over at his dad, laughing to himself. "You know, when Ryan said Ray should become a lawyer, and you kind of agreed? Well, there was another incident last summer when we went on vacation to the Grand Canyon, where I'm thinking we could claim Rayden became our personal family lawyer. At least, that's the way it worked out for the rest of our trip. Like always, while we were gone, I kept getting all these text messages and calls from the lab. It was one of those times when it seemed like nobody could get a handle on the projects they were working on back here. On our second day, after who-knows-how many texts, I think I might have grumbled about it a little under my breath.

"The next time my business phone clanged with a text, Rayden looked up at me with his classic scowl, and said, 'Dad, let me answer it.' So, I asked him if he planned to solve our newest physics dilemma with his best chemical analysis. He nodded and stuck out his hand. Having no idea what he had in mind, I handed him the phone and told him to go ahead, but not to push *Send* until I had a chance to give it my own evaluation—just in case.

"The rest of us sat back and watched, smiling at each other. The scowl on his face as he clicked the keys was worth the whole thing. When he finished, he reread it, took a deep breath, and passed it back to me. I read it and then handed the phone to Madelyn and Ryan and let them both take a look, asking them what they thought—expecting all kinds of sarcasm. By the time it got back to me, one of those two had pushed the send button—not sure which one. They both gave me their best wide-eyed innocent look. Anyway, let me show you the message. I saved it:

LEAVE MY DAD ALONE. He's on vacation. He doesn't NEED ten messages or calls a day so he can tell you people what you should already know. He NEEDS to get away from that place. He NEEDS to relax, have fun, and enjoy life with his family. He'll be back in two weeks. Your problems can wait. Pass the word.

Rayden R. Miller

"As you can see, the response he got was an emoji of a thumb up. Now, you want to know what the best part was? It worked. That was the last I heard from anyone at the office for the rest of our vacation."

Grandpa Watson shook his head, laughing. "Oh boy, he's a character, isn't he?"

Neither Jay nor Madelyn argued the point.

Chapter 13

A couple of days later, Grandpa and the boys were taking a break from the pool and having lunch before he took the two older ones out for their afternoon driving practice. He glanced over at Rayden and Alex, who were scarfing down their PB and J sandwiches and tomato soup. "So, tell me. Are you two leery about flying with me down to Florida this next week? Have you ever been on a plane before?"

Alex wiped his mouth with his sleeve before answering. "Grandpa, we've all been on planes a whole bunch of times— Ray and Ryan especially. With their dad being one of the top science geeks in the world with those weird isotope beam thingies, somebody always wants him to come and bail them out. He won't go more than a day or two unless his family is invited, so they've been all over the world. Fortunately for

Scott and me, during vacation times he includes us a lot. As he puts it, *It's an important part of your education.* All of us have passports and have flown a lot. Personally, I always find it a lot of fun to see and experience new places—not too concerned with the educational part."

Grandpa smiled. "That's good to hear. I wouldn't want either one of you to have a panic attack if we hit a little turbulence." Speaking, he realized there was still a lot about his family he didn't know. That had been the first time he'd heard anything about any of their travels related to Jay's job. He couldn't wait to learn everything.

Rayden laughed. "When we were flying from Germany to New York last summer, we ran into a lot of turbulence, and our plane bounced all over the place. On one really bad bump, some little girl sitting across the aisle from us pumped both of her fists into the air and screamed out, *Yahoo*! It really did kind of break the tension 'cause everyone around us laughed at her."

That resolved one of Grandpa Watson's major concerns. It had also given him a little more information about his son which he hadn't known. Jay had never said a whole lot about his job. He had told him that he was the director of the isotope facility, but hadn't made a big deal out of it. It sounded to him like maybe his son *was* a big deal. He smiled.

The following Friday morning everyone was ready for the trip. As Rob, Jay, and the two older lads packed the car with their suitcases, both dads pulled their younger boys aside. Each handed their son two one-hundred dollar bills.

Jay spoke for the two of them. "Do not let your grandpa spend his money on your meals. Eat healthy and eat lots. You gotta keep your strength up. Remember. Grandpa is not as young as you guys are. It's *your* job to do all the work— packing, moving things around, and lifting. We don't want him having a heart attack or anything, do we?"

"Don't worry, Dad. We've got this. And, oh, by the way, if we eat really cheaply and don't spend all of this loot on food, do we get to keep what's left over for good stuff like chemicals, test tubes, and more important things like that?"

Uncle Rob put his hands on his hips and glared down at the two kids. "No! You either spend it all on food or give what's left back when Uncle Jay and I get there."

"Poor sport," Rayden smirked.

Madelyn, Grandma Roberts, and Rob's wife took Grandpa Watson and the two younger boys to the airport. At the same time they were leaving the house, Jay, Rob, and the two older boys backed out of the driveway and headed out for their own road trip to Florida. Scott was behind the wheel for the first two-hour leg.

Needless to say, the three women felt a tad apprehensive. They had never sent their husbands and sons off on an adventure like that while they stayed home. That morning both moms had fed their boys and husbands big breakfasts, but nerves hadn't done their own appetites any good. They watched as the two younger ones and Grandpa Watson passed through security. When the guys reached the top of the escalator and were ready to disappear down the hall towards their assigned gate, they turned and waved.

The ladies waved back, keeping a couple of tears well-hidden. When the guys were out of sight, the three women looked at each other, wiped their faces, and then walked into the airport restaurant for a quick cup of coffee and chocolate muffin before heading off to work.

The flight was uneventful. The first leg to Detroit only took about a half hour in the air, and then after a change of planes and an hour layover, their aircraft lifted off the runway again. The three of them sat together in the same row on the left side of the aisle. The kids told Grandpa he could have the window. They didn't care. As soon as they were settled, both boys pulled out their e-books and spent most of the flight reading and playing games—except, of course, when they were gabbing about one thing or the other or snacking when the stewardess brought treats.

Grandpa spent a lot of time looking out the window, contemplating about how much his life had changed in the past month. Was he ready to completely say goodbye to his old life? He did have friends at work he wanted to stay in contact with. However, living by himself in an apartment without any family or co-workers nearby after retirement had not been fun. He knew he'd be far happier, leaving to start a new life.

When the threesome arrived in Florida, Grandpa Watson rented a car, and off they went to his home a little over a hundred miles away.

While riding and gaping out of the windows, Rayden spoke up. "Grandpa, I know we don't have a lot of time before the rest of 'um get here, and we've got a lot of work to do, but if there's any way we can see an alligator, I'd love it."

"Me too," Alex said. "Know what? I'd like to see a whale and a shark too."

"Oh, yeah, me too," Rayden said.

Grandpa smiled. "Well, we'll see how our time goes. Not sure about whales and sharks, but I'm pretty sure we can manage an alligator. You know what, Al, just between you and me, if Ray gets too sassy, we'll stop by a pond on the way home and toss him in. Then you and I will get to see a really big one."

"*Grandpa!*" Rayden spouted, pretending to be offended.

Knowing he was joking, all three had a good laugh. Having a jovial new grandpa around was a lot of fun.

On the two-hour trip from the airport to Grandpa's apartment, they stopped for lunch. Starved, the boys ordered half-pound, double cheeseburgers with sweet-potato fries. Grandpa had coffee and a cup of yogurt with berries. When they finished, the boys reached into their pockets and dug out one of the bills their dads had given them for food.

Grandpa took one look and snickered. "Put that away. I'm gonna work your tails off the next couple of days so you're going to *earn* your keep."

Alex looked at his cousin who looked back at him and slowly shook his head. "Grandpa, no. We don't wanna get in trouble with our parents. They told us to pay for our own food. Seems to me like it'd be easier if you held on to our money and paid for our meals out of it?"

"Tell ya what. If I start feeling like I'm headed to the poorhouse because I'm running low on money, I'll take it then. In the meantime, put it back in your pockets, don't lose it, and don't worry about your moms and dads getting angry with you. I'll take care of them. After I tell your parents how hard I made you work, they will probably want me to pay for their meals too."

When they finally got to the house, the three of them stretched out and relaxed a little before getting started. The first thing they did was figure out how to pull the sofa out and turn it into a bed. Once that was completed, Grandpa grabbed sheets and an extra pillow and had the boys give him a hand making it. Then they went into his bedroom and changed the sheets on his bed.

"You two are sleeping together in here. I'll take the sofa bed."

"Grandpa," Rayden said, "We're not gonna take your bed. That's not fair. We're good on the sofa."

Grandpa Watson smiled. He understood their concern so he explained his rationale. "Look, all four of you kids crash between nine-thirty and ten every night. I've been watching you for the past month. I know what you do. Now, I'm different. I always stay up and watch the news from ten to eleven. Then I go to bed. Do you really think you two would find it real restful to be trying to sleep here on the sofa while I have the TV blaring in the background? I don't think so. Besides, it's no big deal for me. I want you comfortable, in bed, and asleep during your normal time—that way I can work your tails off even harder and not feel the least bit guilty about it."

They begrudgingly accepted the plan, even if they didn't feel right about taking his bed while they were there.

Before they could begin packing up the house, they drove
out to one of the big-box stores and bought a stash of 2' x 2'
boxes and tape to seal them shut. Those would be a perfect size
to ship Watson's belongings. As soon as they got back to their
grandpa's condo, the boys and William got to work right away.
First, they cleared a space in the living room to pile the
containers. Then, they went into the kitchen and began boxing
up all the dishes, utensils, cooking ware, pots, pans, and
everything else. After that, they moved to the bathroom,
bedroom, and storage areas throughout the apartment. The only
things they didn't pack were Grandpa's personal items he
would need during the next two or three days.

As planned, the boys did all the manual labor while
Grandpa directed their chores. About six o'clock, Mr. Watson
stopped the work for the day. "Ok, you two. You're both
sweating up a storm. Jump in the shower, change clothes, and
get ready for dinner. We're meeting up with my old boss at the
university at seven o'clock. He's leery that I'm being taken in
by some kind of scam with all of this, so we have to prove him
wrong."

"Why would he think that?" Rayden asked. "Doesn't he believe the DNA test?"

"Oh, yes, he's a pure scientist, but he's also a suspicious type. We'll show him. All he has to do is look at you and me together. Now, get going and get cleaned up."

At seven o'clock when Professor George walked into the restaurant, Grandpa and the boys were already seated. Intentionally, he had made sure that the boys sat on the seats on either side of him—one on his left, one on his right.

Grandpa's old boss took one look at Rayden and said, "Oh, my God. I never would have believed it if I hadn't seen it with my own eyes. That boy looks just like you—only a *year or so* younger."

Everyone else smirked as they looked back and forth at each other.

What really blew Professor George's mind was when Rayden took out his phone and showed him the cropped portraits of William, Jayden, Ryan, and Rayden that his dad had sent to them a month previously, wanting them to pick out which one was Grandpa Watson. After Rayden told him which one was which, the professor no longer had any concerns about

William being taken advantage of in any way. He had found his family.

"This is amazing," the Mr. George said. "I know human genetics can do some wild and crazy things, but I've never seen anything like this. Images of the four of you at the ripe old age of fourteen or fifteen make you look like clones."

Naturally, Alex had to get in on the fun. "As you can obviously see, my brother Scott and I *somehow* got eliminated from the genetic look-alike mix. I guess *somebody* in the family had to improve our looks, so apparently, it's been left up to the rest of us."

As had become the norm, everyone laughed again—even Professor George. Watson had already explained to him the adoptive/step relationship on the other side of the family over the phone, even though he never referred to them in those terms to anyone else. They *were* a part of his new-found family of two sons, their mother along with wives, and four grandsons. He loved them all.

Dinner lasted for almost two hours of talking, laughing, and just plain relaxing and having fun. The day had been long and full. When they finally made it back to Grandpa's apartment, the boys were exhausted. They'd had a busy day. Within a half hour, both were in bed and sound asleep.

After breakfast the next morning, they finished up packing everything that could be boxed. The rest of the items would have to wait until the day they left. There would have to be one last load of laundry done on the final morning, and then those clothes could also be boxed up, finishing the job. Both boys called their dads to report in.

Chapter 14

If anyone on the road drove by them right then and
happened to notice, the scene might have looked a little
confusing. They'd see two adults, one in the front and one in
the back, talking on the phone at the same time, but not the
teenagers. Most anyone driving by who had just happened to
notice would have assumed it to be the other way around.

Whichever boy was driving at the time would have his dad
beside him, so on this leg of the trip, Rob sat in the front
passenger seat, chatting with Alex as Scott drove. At the same
time, Jayden sat in the back seat, gabbing on his phone with
Rayden. Ryan sat beside him—listening, but not talking on his
phone.

One of the reasons for the calls had been to find out when
Rob and Jay thought they would arrive at Grandpa Watson's

house in Florida? As close as anyone could figure, it would be later in the afternoon the next day. The way it worked out, Grandpa, Ray, and Alex had a full day to kill while waiting for them. All the packing that could be done had been completed.

After the call, Grandpa told the two of them to get ready. They were going to leave a little early for lunch. He wanted to do something on the way.

"Have either one of you ever had a massage?" Grandpa asked.

Neither of the boys had. They weren't even 100% sure what one entailed. Their parents didn't get them, and they'd never heard of any of their friends having one either.

Grandpa drove to the mall and parked at the middle door entrance. The three of them climbed out of the car and walked into the shopping center. A short time later, Grandpa led them into this small store front. Three Chinese men stood around the desk by the door. They all recognized Mr. Watson, smiled, and asked if all three would be getting a massage.

Grandpa Watson told them yes and that the boys were new at this, so go "lightly" or "medium," with their kneading, but not "deep." All three would have a thirty minute massage.

The boys had no clue what he was talking about or what to expect but followed whichever man motioned to them. They entered their own private cubical, which had curtains on each side and were open in the front. Both stood there, not knowing what to do.

Each masseuse essentially said the same thing, "Empty your pockets and take off your shoes. Then, lie face down on the table with your nose stuck in the slot. Then, just relax and let me take over. Do you have any muscles that are tight or sore?"

Neither did. They lay quietly and relaxed while the masseuse worked them over for a half hour. During the experience, the men asked more than once if the boys were OK or if they were kneading too hard. Both were fine with what was happening. When they were done, the men tapped the boys on the shoulders and told them, "All done." Then he took hold of one of their arms to stabilize them as the boys swung their legs over the table and stood. It had been quite a new experience for both.

Grandpa slipped the person at the desk his credit card and paid. Neither boy could get a glimpse of what it cost, and both knew they probably didn't want to find out. Again, they offered to pay and again were told to put their money away.

On their way out of the mall as they crossed the parking lot, headed to the car, Grandpa asked, "Well, what'd you think? Would you do it again?"

"Yeah," Rayden said. "I gotta admit it though, there was one time he freaked me out for just a second until I figured out what he was doing. Then I was OK."

Alex looked at him and smiled. "When he jammed his elbow down to the bone on your butt cheek?"

"Yeah,"

"That kind of creeped me out too. Never had anyone play with my butt before," Alex said.

Grandpa laughed. "He wasn't *playing* with your bottom. There are a lot of muscles in there that get stiff and affect your stride and posture while walking. Besides, let's face it that feels a lot better than getting the thing swatted."

The smile vanished from Rayden's face. I've never been hit by either one of my parents—ever!"

"Me either," said Alex. "That doesn't mean I don't have my bedroom ceiling memorized from being sent to my room."

"None of us get punished too often, and I still think the last time I did was a rip-off," Rayden said.

Grandpa smiled, as he unlocked the car and everyone got in. He couldn't imagine Madelyn or Jay punishing the kids unfairly. He was both amused and curious. Before starting the car, he asked, "So, what did you do that was so terrible, Ray, where you had to stare at your bedroom ceiling for hours on end when you were totally innocent?"

"Well, to be completely honest, I wasn't *totally innocent*, but it wasn't that big a deal. Dad caught me sneaking around and turning off his business phone one night so I got sent to bed an hour early. The bad part is, I think he set me up—again."

"So, before we head out, tell me the whole story," Grandpa said. "Why would you turn off his phone?"

"You know, I'm very proud of my dad and love him to pieces. The more I've learned about him and his determination to succeed in life and be the very best in his field, considering everything he had to put up with in his younger years blows me away. I just wish he wasn't so darned well known in the physics world. We can't go anyplace or do anything without that phone ringing constantly. We can't go to a ball game or watch a movie on TV without the stupid thing clanging away."

"So, how'd that get you into trouble?" Grandpa asked.

"One night after dinner, when we'd gotten back from our bike rides, the day was about done. We'd all settled down for the evening, I love that time of night when our family's all sitting around together doing nothing but talking, reading, watching TV, and letting down.

"However, his business phone never quits, so he has to get up, go out into the kitchen where we stash all our phones during dinner, and answer it. So I started a little habit of roaming around the house, getting a quick drink of water, going to the bathroom, whatever, and sneakily turning it off when he wasn't looking. Well, one night, he slipped up behind me when I went into the kitchen. He caught me red handed. He yelled at me for a couple of seconds, and then sent me to bed— *to think about things*."

"So, why do you think that was such cruel and unusual punishment?" Grandpa asked, smiling.

"Two reasons," Rayden said. "First off's the fact that he sneaked around and followed me, catching me in the act was cheating. And then, secondly, ever since that night, he's been turning it off himself during dinner and leaving it off. So, I think I was right after all and shouldn't have gotten yelled at or sent to bed early."

Grandpa Watson and Alex both laughed at that one.

"What you're saying then is maybe the extra hour of sleep you got that night was worth it in the end?" Grandpa said.

Rayden smiled and shrugged his shoulders without answering.

"Hey! Let's face it, we're the kids. Sometimes we just can't win," Alex said.

"Yeah," Grandpa said, "but sometimes you do. From the way I see it, Ray's stunts have won for him twice that I know of. Your Uncle Jay showed me a text message that Ray sent from the Grand Canyon on his phone dealing with the same topic that also worked perfectly."

"Dad showed you that? I can't believe he saved it," Rayden said.

"Yep, he did. However, I think it's time for lunch," Grandpa said, starting the car. "And, we're going to go to one of my favorite spots so you two need to start thinking about what you're hungry for. They have some really good fried shrimp there if you're into that kind of thing."

Lunch, full of laughter and chatter, lasted about an hour. The boys ate well—they always did. Not one more word was mentioned about any of Rayden's shenanigans with his dad's cell phone.

After lunch, Grandpa told them he had something else to show them. He drove to a park several miles from his house. It took about a half hour traveling time. When they got out of the car, he told them to follow him. There was an extension bridge completely covered with heavy-duty fencing so there was no way anyone could fall off the bridge and into the water. There were a number of other sightseers walking on the bridge so it swayed slightly with all the foot traffic.

On the other side of the stream, they spotted several gators sunning themselves. As they walked across the overpass, they also saw four or five ducklings floating in the water. Grandpa told them, "Watch for eyes just above above the water line."

They didn't see any eyes, but suddenly a huge head with open jaws burst out of the water and inhaled one of the young ducks.

"Whoa!" yelled Rayden in tune to all kinds of screams, screeches, and other reactions from the rest of the people on the bridge. "Did you see that?"

One doesn't have to have a great imagination to know what that evening's dinner conversation consisted of. Both boys were *very* excited, and talked nonstop. Grandpa listened and enjoyed the chatter. He had a plan for the next day.

Chapter 15

After Jayden, Rob, and the two older boys arrived, they finished packing all but the last minute stuff, shipped all the packages, and then had the rest of the day free before leaving the next morning. Grandpa told the boys that he wanted to show them his workplace. The truth was, Grandpa Watson wanted to take his family to the robotics lab at the university to show them off. He also needed to sign some last-minute paperwork. He had already introduced his ex-boss to the two younger boys, so now he wanted to show the rest of the family off to his friends and former co-workers. They all knew about the recent phenomenon in his life, but hadn't seen the living proof.

When they walked into the lab, Mr. Watson told his family to look around while he went into the office to sign the documents. The university needed his new contact information. As the robotics laboratory had been his brain child, they were constantly calling on him for help and advice even though he was supposed to be retired. And, everyone understood it would continue even after he left the state.

"William, I need you to look at something for me," one of the lab managers said as he walked up to Jayden.

Jay smiled and turned to face him. "Uh, I'm Jayden Miller, William's son."

The man's jaw dropped as he looked at the six people one-at-a-time. "Wow! William told us all about how much some of you looked so much alike. But, I never thought it would be like this. Sorry about the mix-up. I saw you, and just assumed you were William."

Jay told him he had no problem with the mistake and then introduced his brother, sons, and nephews.

The lab manager looked at Ryan and Rayden. "Mr. Watson didn't' tell us you were identical twins, he just said that four of you looked a lot alike."

Ryan slipped up beside his brother, "We're a year apart. I'm almost an inch taller."

"He's also the biggest troublemaker," Rayden said with a straight face. "As you can see, the only thing I have going for me is that I'm by far the better looking one of two of us."

The rest of the family snorted, coughed, and laughed—again.

"OK, I see one of you is taller now—don't know about the troublemaker part—or who is better looking, but wait a minute, I just thought of something. Didn't William tell us that one of the four of you is a robotics geek? Which one of you is it?" He suddenly had an idea. Maybe he could have some fun picking on his co-workers.

The other five in the family all pointed at Ryan, who smiled and then said, "We're all STEM. Rayden is science, I'm technology, Scott is engineering, and Alex is math. So, yeah, I'm the one who loves robots."

"OK, you're Ryan, right?" the manager said, looking around as some of the other engineers gathered around.

Ryan nodded.

"If that's the case, Ryan, would you be willing to look at one of our machines while your grandpa is tied up? We've been waiting for William to make an appearance so we could stick him with the chore. We have a new robot that acts real herky-jerky. We can't get it to run smoothly."

"I can take a look," Ryan said, "but Grandpa is probably the one who should."

His answer surprised the lab manager as well as all of the other engineers. Not a one of them expected he'd be willing to try. He really expected Ryan to back off and freak out a little.

"Well, nobody else around here can figure it out, so I'm thinking why not giving William's grandson a shot at it. Since he's the family's other robotics genius, maybe he can spot something amiss."

By that time, everyone around the place, except Ryan, knew he was picking on the engineers. No way could a teenager fix the problem.

"We think it has to do with the programming," the manager said, once again looking wide-eyed at the handful of programmers gathered around. "Here, Ryan, sit down, and I'll turn on the robot and the monitor. That way you can look at all the coding as the robot goes through its motions. See if you can spot anything that doesn't look right to you."

The technician ran the robot through its paces for a couple of minutes. It caught on every movement to the left.

While everyone else stood around behind Ryan's back and watched the robot go through its paces, Ryan stared at the screen while the others grinned at one another, thinking, *Yeah, right. The kid's got this.*

A few moments later, as Ryan continued to study the code on the monitor, Grandpa walked up behind him, placed his hands on Ryan's shoulders, kneading them and his neck.

Ryan scrunched his shoulders and squirmed, not once taking his eyes off the code.

Grandpa laughed and removed his hands. "I guess I'm bugging you. Sorry about that."

"No, no," Ryan said, without looking away from the screen. "Don't stop, please. Feels so good. Love it."

"He's the squirmer," Jayden said. "He does the same thing when I walk up behind him and massage his back and neck when he's at his computer. Rayden doesn't. He just sits there ignoring me, like I'm not even there."

"Grandpa," Ryan said as he started to stand. "You're the one who should be down here, not me."

"Stay there. You're fine," Grandpa said. "Have you ever seen a problem like this before?"

"Yes, it's a lot like the hitch I had on my own robot."

"Do you remember what you did to fix it?" Grandpa asked.

"Yeah, you showed me."

"But you did the work, so transfer what you learned there to this problem."

"I think it's right here," Ryan said. "This code looks scrambled to me. What do you think I should do?"

"What do *you* think you should do," Grandpa said. "You're the one fixing the problem."

Ryan looked up with a wry smile and then babbled a ton of coding jargon to his grandpa, which nobody else in the group understood.

"So, try it and see if it works," Grandpa said.

"But, I don't want to mess it up."

"You can't. It's been saved. If it isn't right, we can push the reset, and the code will return to what it is now."

"Don't you think you should be the one doing this, Grandpa?"

"Nope. Go for it."

So he did. For the next few minutes Ryan switched coding dialogue all over the screen. When he finished, he looked up. "Will it work?"

"I don't know," Grandpa said. "Will it?"

"Only one way to find out," Ryan said. "I guess we'll have to turn the machine back on and see if the jerking motion is still there."

They did and the robot ran perfectly—not one irregular movement to be seen.

Mr. Watson looked over at the lab director who had also joined the group. "What do you think? Should we save what he did?"

Wide-eyed, the executive reached over and pushed the save button. Then, he said, "Yes! That thing has never run like that—ever." Then he looked Ryan in the eye. "How old are you, young man?"

"I'm fifteen," Ryan said, standing and stepping away from the screen.

"When you are ready to go to college, you let me know, and I'll make sure you get a free ride right here. So, what grade are you in now?"

"I'm a freshman in high school, but, as far a college goes, I bleed Green and White."

"Keep my card," he said, pulling one out of his wallet and handing it to Ryan. "If you change your mind between now and then, let me know.

In the meantime, the other programmers, who had gathered behind Ryan and the monitor while watching, were staring back and forth between Ryan, the monitor, and the robot in complete disbelief of what they had just witnessed.

The manager who had put Ryan up to the task moved to the front of the crowd. "People, I have a confession to make. I asked Ryan to sit down and look at the robot and its coding as a joke. I never expected for him to even look at it, much less fix the problem.

"Ryan, you shocked me to pieces when you agreed to take a look—even though you thought your grandpa *should* be the one to do it. Not only did you have the self confidence as a fifteen-year-old to look, but you spotted the problem and fixed it. No way in my wildest dreams did this end up the way I expected. Congratulations, and I hope you change your mind and join us when you graduate from high school."

After that, formal introductions were made between the lab's director who had pushed the *save* button and Dr. Watson's family, and then William gave them a tour of the facility.

As they prepared to leave, the director slipped up to William one last time. "What kind of students are they overall? Do you know?"

"Yeah, Jay and Rob both showed me their kids' report cards online. Jay told me that he thought there just might be a never-mentioned competition running among them—who would get the first B?"

"All A's, huh?"

"Yep, and apparently, not a one of them is willing to change the trend. According to Jay, all four of them work their tails off in school. They are all great kids and great students in that order."

Chapter 16

When the family left the university, there was still considerable time left in the day. Grandpa Watson had a plan. He stopped Jay and Rob before they got into their cars. The four boys had already crawled in—Scott behind the steering wheel of Jay's car with Ryan in the back. Alex and Rayden were in Grandpa's. Like their older brothers, they also took turns riding in the front passenger seat.

"The younger ones have already seen an alligator," Mr. Watson said. "But, one of them indicated he'd love to see a whale as well. The closest whale watch is almost an hour away. They have an afternoon tour which lasts from four to six. What do you think?"

Rob looked at Jayden, "I think the timing is perfect," Rob said. "Then, we could grab a bite to eat, get back and get a decent night's sleep before heading out in the morning."

"Works for me," Jay said. "What's the address? We'll punch it into our GPS."

Everything worked to perfection. Not only did they see whales, seals, and sharks, but on the way back they spotted a giant alligator sunning itself on the side of the road.

Amid all the chatter at dinner, Jayden's dad, suddenly appeared somber, looked back and forth between Jay and Rob, catching their attention. "Do you think we could make one last stop after dinner before calling it a night?"

"Sure," Rob said. "Where you want to go?"

"I have this friend—acquaintance, who is living at the senior center. I'd like to stop in and visit for a minute and show off my family. Think we could do that?"

Jay caught the sudden change in his dad's demeanor, and it spiked his curiosity. "I don't know why not. So, who is this guy? I don't think we've ever heard about him, have we?"

"You haven't. Thirty-eight years ago, as a brand new detective on the local police force, he investigated your abduction day and night. Even though it eventually became a cold case, in his mind, it always remained active." Mr. Watson paused for a moment, appearing deep in thought.

"So, the two of you have kept in contact all this time?" Jayden said.

"Yes, he and I have talked many, many times over the years. Each and every time he thought he'd found something new, he'd come and tell me about it. And, then, when the latest lead turned out to be another dead end, he always let me know about that that as well."

"So, what's the problem?" Jay asked.

"I really don't know. He's getting older and more fragile, and I don't know how he's going to handle this. He's always felt like he was a failure because he couldn't solve the crime. However, one way or the other, I have to let him know about our reconnecting. I realize it sounds ridiculous, but I've been debating with myself for weeks on how to do it. I could probably just call him, but I'd much rather show him. Whichever way we do it, I don't want him hurt in any way."

Rob looked at Jay and then back at William. "You're right. You need to let him see this genetic phenomenon in person, so I'm thinking that it probably should be you, Jay, and his two boys who go. Me and my brood can stay at your place and kick back while you're gone."

"No, I want all of us to visit him. The three of you are my family too."

Twenty minutes later, the seven of them walked into the game room at the senior center. Sergeant McAlson was playing cards with a group of friends and didn't notice them walking towards him.

One of the card players did. He looked back and forth between William, Jay, Ryan, and Rayden who were walking as a group only slightly separated from Rob and his kids. "Whoa! Am I seeing double or quadruple?"

The rest of the men at the table turned to look. Sergeant McAlson pushed back his chair and stood. He knew without being told who he was looking at.

After introductions were made around the table, he took the family group back to his room to talk in private. Twenty minutes later, after a quick re-telling of the past years, the group readied to leave. Before walking out the door, Rayden looked up at Officer McAlson. "Is that creep still in jail?"

McAlson looked at William uncomfortably, hoping for some help. "I don't know if I should tell you boys about this or not. Let's face it, you might be a little young for this story. William, what do you think? You know all the details. Are they ready for this?"

"Mac, I have no idea what *details* you're talking about. Because of everything going on with Caroline at the time, as soon as he was convicted and sent to prison, I completely wiped that man out of my mind."

Jayden looked over at his brother before speaking. "What do you think, Rob? They've all read mystery and crime novels. I doubt if any gory details they might hear would shock them too badly. Besides, I'm curious myself."

"I've got no problem with it, go ahead and let us in on the whole story."

Mac looked back and forth among the seven people standing by the door getting ready to leave. "First off, thirty-eight years ago things were a lot different than they are today. Security cameras were not nearly as plentiful, and people were able to do a lot of bad things without nearly as much fear of being caught. Not only that, but a lot of crimes committed in prison were hidden within the organization. A lot of what happened then was never reported to anyone outside of the system. It wasn't like today when some politician gives someone a dirty look, and it's national news within five minutes."

"So, what happened to the dude who kidnapped my dad?" Rayden snarled.

"Ray, tone of voice," Jayden murmured to his son.

"I'm sorry, Mr. McAlson, please go on with the story."

Mac looked back and forth between William and the boys' dads, still not sure if he wanted to tell everything. "William, I can't believe you never heard about this—even though news of this kind was kept secret within prison walls whenever possible. I guess I'm even more surprised that I never told you. Anyway, boys, there are two types of criminals who many times don't last very long in prison—child molesters and kidnappers of young children. Do any of you four know what a shiv is?"

Alex looked up and spoke immediately. "Isn't that a homemade dagger or knife? I read a story one time where a guy had a big plastic spoon and sharpened it into a knife and stabbed somebody with it."

"I thought that was called a shank," Ryan said.

"You're both right," McAlson said. "A shiv and a shank are the same—a homemade knife or weapon. Anyway, to get back to the story, within three months of the time Jayden's kidnapper landed in prison, he was found dead in the corner of a shower with a homemade weapon still in him. Someone had stabbed him in his lower belly area and then reefed the shiv upwards until it penetrated his heart."

Comments were muttered among the seven spectators along with quizzical looks.

Suddenly, a muffled but clear, "Rayden!" was heard by everyone in the crowd.

"Wha…, what, Dad? I didn't say anything."

"You didn't have to. Unfortunately for you, you've always worn your emotions on your face, and I'm not happy with what I just saw."

Rayden walked over and wrapped his arm around his dad and leaned into him. "Can't help it, Dad. I love you so much. I'm glad the guy got what he deserved."

Without another word, Jayden wrapped his arm around Ray and held him tightly.

Shortly afterwards the meeting broke up and the seven visitors left Officer McAlson's apartment.

After walking to their cars with them and saying their goodbyes, McAlson smiled again. "I *will* call the office tomorrow and let them know. It's time to close the Watson abduction file."

After all the final handshakes, the family headed out. The boys especially needed to get some sleep. The next couple of days would be tedious.

With everything shipped and the last minute bed-stripping and final packing done, the five of them hit up the local restaurant William frequented for breakfast, said his goodbyes to the wait staff, and off they drove, headed for Michigan. Giving the two teenage drivers appropriate rest breaks, the trip would take another two-and-a-half days.

When the two cars eventually pulled into Jay's driveway, Madelyn, Mom Roberts, and Rob's wife stepped out to greet them. Hugs and kisses passed among them. Their guys were home at last.

That night, Grandpa Watson slept in his new home for the first time. They'd brought all of his personal effects with them in the car, so it was no big problem. As soon as the shipping company arrived and dropped off the packages, Grandpa called the boys, and they hustled over to help. After he opened the boxes, he told the kids where to put them. The four teens carried them to the appropriate rooms, so they completed the job quickly. Grandpa took over from there and unpacked at his leisure.

After emptying the cases and putting most everything away and settling in, William spent the next afternoon going through his papers. He shredded old and no longer needed documents. However, one of the papers he found, he did not destroy. Staring at William Ward Watson, Jr.'s birth certificate brought back too many memories.

When William, Sr. gave Jayden his original birth certificate, he did it in private. "You know, Jay, this does bring up some issues. Every single official document you own has your incorrect birth date."

"Name too, if you want to get technical about it," Jayden said.

"Just out of curiosity, what have you always used for your birthday?" William asked.

"The original Jayden's. In reality, I'm two months younger than he would have been."

"Ever think our reconnecting could cause so many problems?" William smiled.

"I don't really consider them problems," Jayden said. "I guess I just see them as issues that have to be dealt with."

That same evening, as the family sat around the living room after dinner, Jayden brought up his concerns to his family. "OK, everyone, let's talk seriously about something. I have two names—one my legal birth name, and another one, the name given to me when I was abducted. I'm conflicted. Need your input."

William set down his e-reader and spoke first. "During your lifetime, you were William for two months, and since then you've been Jayden for thirty-eight years. I think it's a no-brainer. Your name now and always will be Jayden Scott Miller. However, I do think you need to do something about *legalizing* it, possibly by getting a new and revised birth certificate showing your name and your actual birth date. I'm assuming Rob could aim you in the right direction. Even though his specialty is corporate law, he more than likely knows somebody who could take care of it."

"So, I think I probably should use the birth date on *William, Jr's* birth certificate."

"Yes," William said. "For social security, Medicare, retirement, marriage license, passport, and all that, everything should be accurate. You certainly wouldn't want to retire someday and learn you couldn't collect all your benefits because your birth date didn't match the official records. People change their names all the time, but not their birth dates."

Ryan looked back and forth at his dad and grandpa. "Does that mean my last name is also legally Watson? Will Ray and I have to do anything to keep our names as we've always known them?"

"No, you're fine," Jayden said. "Ryan Scott Miller is the name you were given when you were born. It's on your birth certificate that way, so there's no problem with the two of you."

"Good. I've got nothing against the name Watson, but changing everything would be a disaster. Never thought of it before, but think about what a lady has to go through when she gets married and changes her last name. That would have to be tough."

"That's totally different, honey." Madelyn smiled. "And, I think most women look forward to the change under the circumstances. However, did you know many women don't change their last names when they marry?"

"I think the hardest part for me, then, will be getting used to a new birthday." Jayden said. "It's been in July forever."

Rayden had held his tongue for as long as he could. "Dad, you're way over-thinking this. Make it simple and keep both birthdays—one in July and one in September. It'll give you two special days, two birthday cakes, two days when Ry and I will bow down to your every wish and whim, and *maybe—just maybe*, you might even get two presents. Of course, flipping the coin to its other side, having those two birthdays a year means you're actually seventy-six instead of thirty-eight."

"Oh, brother," Jayden groaned as everyone else laughed.

Chapter 17

After all the drama, changes, and readjustments of the past
few months, life had pretty-much gotten back to normal. One
rainy and windy Sunday afternoon that fall, all ten family
members sat around the dining room table instead of on the
patio where they normally ate their weekly dinner together. As
they were finishing up and waiting for dessert, the boys started
squirming a bit. Watching them, Grandma snickered. She
figured they were thinking they'd heard enough chatter. It was
past time to cut the pies.

However, before she did, she discovered that wasn't the
reason for their apparent unease. Rob, who had also noticed
Rayden sneaking sly glances at him with a silly grin on his face
spoke up. "Alright, Ray-Ray, what's going on? Uncle Rob's
getting suspicious."

"Um…" Rayden paused, scanning the faces of his older brother and cousins. All three smiled and each one nodded a single time—their cue. He'd been elected—again. "We've got a question."

"Shoot!"

"Well, you know, because of everything that's happened around here in the past few months, we've heard a lot of things about yours and Dad's childhoods we've never known about before—both good and bad stuff when it comes to Dad. With you, it's been mostly good. Some of the goofy things you and Dad did together were actually pretty funny, and we'd like to hear about *another* story."

"Um, if we're going back into the *Dark Ages*, as you four so often refer to our childhood, you're going to have to quit beating around the bush and get a little more detailed," Rob said, wondering what those four were up to this time.

"For some reason-or-the-other, it seems like *maybe* we've *somehow* also discovered another incident that happened to *you* back in those days, which we want to know a little more about."

Ray's comments had pretty much caught everyone's attention. Conversations around the table ceased, and the rest of the family zeroed in on the two of them—listening, watching, and waiting, all wondering the same thing, *now what?*

"Okay, I'll bite," Rob said, unable to stifle his grin. "What on earth are you talking about this time?"

"I've heard that *maybe* there was an incident back in your high school days where *you* earned *double* extra credit points in English class one time when you and Dad worked on a haiku project together. Now, c'mon, how is that even fair if you guys created a project together, and you ended up with twice the points? I can't believe that Dad didn't do his share of the work. What's the story here?"

Five of the six adults, sitting around the table, burst into laughter—joined by the smirks on the four teens' faces. Grandpa Watson had no clue what was going on, but couldn't help but smile, wondering to himself, *oh, boy, what's this one all about?* It seemed like he learned something new and different about his family almost every day. He couldn't wait to hear about this one.

"Alright, Ray, who told you about my extra credit coup?" Rob asked, still laughing.

"Can't tell you who told *me*," Rayden said. "But, if you put your mind to it, I think you could probably whittle it down to either a brother or a cousin who *might* have heard a rumor about it from one of those three really old people still hanging out at the high school."

Mom Roberts interrupted the conversation, smiling as usual. "Rob, I'm not sure if you should tell these characters the story about that one or not. I certainly wouldn't want them trying anything as ridiculous as that was."

"Mom, you know they're way smarter than we were at their age. I'm sure they wouldn't pull a stunt like that—unless, of course, they *really* do love staring at their bedroom ceilings for hours at a time." With that, he gave his sons and nephews *the look.*

Then, Rob glanced over to his brother, hoping for a little help. All he got from Jay was a grin and his right arm held straight out, palm up. It was up to him.

"Okay, okay, I'll tell you the story. It all started during the last hour on a Friday afternoon. Mr. Grossman, our English teacher, had given us the last twenty minutes or so to finish up anything that needed to be done before the weekend started.

"When there was about a minute left in the period before the bell rang, he interrupted us as we were gathering up all our stuff so we could race for the door. He reminded us that we didn't have any homework in his class for the weekend, so he was giving us a chance to earn some extra credit. We'd been working on haikus the past few days, so he made us a deal. If we were able to come up with a haiku that we could *demonstrate*, he'd see if he couldn't come up with ten extra credit points. He emphasized that he didn't mean just any old three random lines consisting of the five-seven-five syllable count, but something that created an image the class could visualize in their minds. It had to be both written and displayed to the class.

"When the bell rang, Jay and I walked out the door, took our shortcut through the gym, and strolled out to the parking lot, gabbing away as always. We were free for the weekend. Nobody else had given us any homework either—which had to be a record of some kind. Anyway, with football season over, there were no games, no practices, nothing for once that *had* to be done. Nothing, that is, but goof off the whole weekend and enjoy ourselves.

"I'm sure the biggest worry in our lives that afternoon was whether or not your grandma had left us anything good to snack on when we got home. Believe it or not, there were times in those days when there were no cookies, pie, or cake to be found after school. Can you imagine that? Horrors!"

The boys laughed. How many times had they slipped by Grandma's for their after school snacks when they knew there was nothing good to eat at home? She always had something.

Rob continued his story. "As you know, back in those days Grandma was a registered nurse for a pediatrician in private practice. However, there were times when the hospital had a personnel shortage of some kind, so she'd get called in to help out at the pediatric emergency ward. So, it just so happened that Saturday morning, the hospital called and asked if she could come in and cover for somebody for a while—not all day, but maybe six hours at most. Jay and I would be on our own—with *nobody* looking over our shoulders.

"So, while your dad and I were eating breakfast, he looked over at me from the sports page he'd been reading—along with absorbing his second bowl of cereal, and smirked. When he got that particular look on his face, it usually meant trouble. Then he told me he'd been thinking about the extra credit haiku assignment, and that he had an idea.

"*Oh no,*" I remember thinking to myself. "*Do I want to hear this?* He still had that goofy grin.

"He looked me up and down and then commented about how much bigger I was than him. Then he asked me if he made his body ramrod stiff, did I think I could lift him over my head and strut across the room bellowing out a haiku he'd dreamed up?

"I laughed and told him I could grab him by the belt and lift his scrawny butt off the floor one handed. Of course I could hold him over my head.

"How much did you outweigh Uncle Jay back in high school," Alex asked.

"Oh, probably sixty pounds give or take a couple."

"Were you a lot taller then, too?" Ryan asked.

"Maybe six inches, not really sure. We never paid a whole lot of attention to our size differences—at least I didn't, so I don't know exactly. You know, everybody's different.

"Anyway, to get back to the story, your dad said that since Mom wasn't home, maybe we could practice a little and see if we could make it work. He wasn't sure which way would be easier, if I picked him up and held him around the waist or at the hips. We'd have to experiment.

"And we did. First off, he showed me the haiku that he had written. It was simple, so I memorized the fool thing real quick. Then we started trying to figure out how to make our presentation work—we did. Of course, we still had to practice it all weekend—without your grandmother seeing or finding out what we were up to. That took a little sneakiness."

Jay laughed, "Oh, yes. And, boys, the best part of this story hasn't even started yet. Continue on, Bro. This is where the saga gets good."

"Okay," Rob said. "On Monday, as we walked down the hall to go to lunch, I nudged Jay with my elbow and asked him if he wanted to practice one last time before we pulled that baby off for Grossman seventh hour? After all, the theme of the haiku had been geared towards lunch, so why not?

"He looked at me kind of funny. Then he asked me if we really wanted to do it right there in front of the whole school?

"I told him, yeah, it'd be a riot. So, we moved over by the wall where we wouldn't get run over by the mob while we set it up. Jay stood ramrod straight, faced forward, and made his body as stiff as possible. Then, I leaned down,

wrapped my hands around his waist and hoisted him as
high as I could above my head with my arms locked at the
elbows. By then, all the kids in the hallway had started to
gather around, laughing, watching, and wondering what we
were up to. As soon as we were steady and perfectly
balanced, I strutted down the hall towards the lunchroom,
yelling loudly enough so anyone within fifty feet of us
could hear.

HEY! WE'RE COMIN' THROUGH.
MOVE YOUR BUTTS OUT OF OUR WAY.
WE'VE GOT LUNCH TO DO.

Everyone in the family sitting around the table laughed.
"So, then what happened?" Ryan asked.

"That was when things fell apart. Unknown to us at the
time, at the end of the hall by the office windows, which
just happened to also be the edge of the lunch room, stood
our counselor, Mr. Martin, and the school's substitute
security officer. When they heard me yelling out our haiku

over and over, along with all of the laughter from the kids, it *somehow* caught their attention. As they looked up to see what was going on, they saw us headed their way.

"Martin looked over at the policeman and said, 'Oh, no. What are those two dingbats up to now? C'mon, Sarge, we've gotta stop this before somebody gets hurt.'"

"How'd you know that's what they said," Rayden asked. "You couldn't have heard them from where you were."

"No, one of our classmates had stopped to watch when he heard the commotion and just happened to be standing right beside them. He told me what they said later.

"So, then the two of them stormed down the hall towards us. Even over all the noise and laughter in the hall, I heard Mr. Martin yelling at me to put Jay down right then and to be careful.

"Of course, by that time, my adrenalin was pumping big time, so I asked him where the trashcan was so I could throw him in it.

"For some reason or the other, Martin had not gotten into the spirit of the thing. He yelled at me, to quit acting like an idiot and set him down, and to *not* drop him! He said if Jay fell from there and landed on his head, it could kill him.

"Not believing what I was hearing, I shook my head and called back, 'Oh, c'mon, Mr. Martin, I'm not going to drop him. We've practiced this dozens of times'"

"Don't remember the exact words that shrieked out of his mouth, but he *might* have sworn at me—wouldn't bet my life on it, but I do think he called me a bad word. Anyway, I stopped so I could let him down. Standing perfectly still, I tilted my head upwards and asked Jay if he were ready. He told me he was, so, I lowered him slowly down, resting his lower back on my right shoulder and paused for a second, just like we'd practiced time after time. Then I wrapped my arm around his waist and stopped again. When I felt like I had a solid grip, I asked him one more time if he were ready.

"He was, so I squatted down, bent at the knees and leaned over at the waist at the same time, holding on tightly. When Jay touched down on both feet, facing straight ahead, and I knew he was standing upright and steady, I let go."

"So, it all worked out, and nobody fell and got hurt, so everything was good," Ryan said, looking at his dad for confirmation.

Jay smiled at his son and then nodded."More or less," he said.

"Well, almost, Rob continued. Except for the fact that right about then, your dad could see who was in front of us for the first time—the substitute security officer. 'Oops, we're busted,' he said. 'This is the policeman who took me on my driver's test when I got my license a couple of weeks ago. Officer, this is my big brother, Rob, who I told you about'"

"The cop and I nodded at each other, and then the officer looked at Jay and snarled, 'And, here I *thought* you were sane.'

"I know I should've kept my mouth shut, but I couldn't help it. I nudged Jay and whispered aloud, 'By sane, does he mean *out* or *in*?'"

"Being a smart you-know-what, Jay whispered back that the cop must have meant 'out' because no way would anyone consider us *insane*,

"Outsane? What the heck is that?" Rayden asked.

"Just a stupid play on words—insane versus outsane," Jayden said. "We were pumped up and being silly."

Rob continued, "As could be expected, Mr. Martin was not amused. He yelled at us again, 'Don't you two clowns ever pull a stunt like that again. If you'd dropped him on this marble flooring, you could have maimed him for life, if not worse.'"

"Maybe right then I was feeling a little offended, because I think maybe I might have protested a bit, because I kind of snarled when I told him once again that I had a good grip on Jay, and I *knew* I wouldn't drop him. We'd been practicing the thing all weekend, and we *knew* what we're doing,

"I don't know if it was because he picked up on my attitude, but this time the policeman joined the conversation, 'With that horde of kids racing down the hall for lunch, what if somebody had accidentally bumped into you, making you lose your balance? Then what?'

"I guess the reality of it kind of hit me then, because suddenly I thought perhaps our stunt hadn't been such a great idea after all. I admitted, that maybe he was right. We hadn't even thought of that possibility'

"Mr. Martin didn't help things right then when he asked, 'And, what does Mrs. Roberts think of this brilliant stunt?'

"Both of us might have paled a little right then and looked at each other. Finally, Jay answered for the two of us, sheepishly, 'She doesn't know a thing about it, and we're *not* telling her.'

"Martin, shook his head slowly before answering. 'I'm giving you boys two choices. You can bring me a hand-written and signed note tomorrow morning from your mom *before* school starts letting me know you've told her the *entire* story, or I will call her myself during first hour. Got it?'

"Yes, sir! both of us answered him in unison.

"With his hands on his hips, Martin glared at us for a second, and then snarled, 'Get yourselves to lunch while there's still something to eat besides soda crackers and cottage cheese. And, boys, NEVER AGAIN! I mean it.'

"We turned and raced to the rear of the lunch line while the getting was good. We'd had enough chewing out for one day—that is, until we told your grandma when she got home."

"So, after all that happened, how'd you end up getting your extra credit?" Scott asked.

"Yeah, and you said you even got twice as much as Uncle Jay," Alex said. "How'd that work if you couldn't do it anymore?"

"As could be expected, by the time we walked into our seventh hour English class, everyone in school knew about our caper—including Mr. Grossman.

"After he took attendance, he looked around the room with a blank expression before saying anything. Then, he said he wanted to get the class started that afternoon with our extra credit assignments. He wanted those of us who had done them to raise our hands.

"Maybe half a dozen kids held up their hands. Then, one-at-a-time, all of them stood, read, and explained their haikus. Neither Jay nor I even looked up when he walked past us, collecting the written copies. When he returned to the front of the class, he slipped the sheets of paper into the in-basket on his desk, turned, and looked back and forth between Jay and me. 'What gives, guys? I've heard all kinds of rumors today that the two of you have created a very demonstrable haiku, yet you didn't present it to the class or hand in your written copies for extra credit? Why?'

"Naturally, the whole class cracked up over his comments. I waited a second before answering—hoping Jay would. Since he wouldn't even look up, I finally replied. 'Because we can't do it now. Mr. Martin threatened us with our lives if we ever did it again'

"Still keeping a straight face, he responded, 'Now, if I've heard the story correctly, I think he was talking about your doing it on the marble hallways. My classroom floor is wooden, so if Jay falls, it might only knock some sense into at least one of you.'

"I took a deep breath before responding. I didn't want to yell or sound like I felt—like, nobody trusted us. 'I won't drop him. Like I told Mr. Martin over and over again, we *know* what we're doing. We've practiced it too many times not to.'

"'Okay,' Mr. Grossman said. 'Let me close the door, and then you two come up here in front and show me and the class your haiku'.

"So, what could we do? Jay and I walked to the front of the room, and demonstrated our poetic masterpiece, complete with my vocal presentation—only, not quite as loudly as I had done in the hallway. I did manage, however, to screw up my face with a slightly goofy expression as I strutted across the room, much to the delight of our classmates. When we finished, we once again went through our dismount routine, which, just like we knew it would, worked perfectly.

Grossman smiled when we finished, probably relieved because I hadn't dropped him. So, then he asked if during our practice sessions, we'd tried any different ways of doing it?

"I told him we had. For the most part our experiments had to do with where I held on to him when I picked him up off the floor. When I grabbed him around the waist, it pinched him a bit and kind of hurt. Yet, when I lifted him from Maddie's petting zone, it was more comfortable for him, but he didn't feel quite as balanced or steady. So, we decided to stick to the waist lift.

"Mr. Grossman looked back and forth between us. Then he asked, 'Do I even dare ask about *Maddie's petting zone*?'

Grandpa Watson may not have known what Rob was talking about, but everyone else sitting around the dining room table listening to the story did.

Madelyn piped up, "Rob, do you have to?"

"Yeah," he said. "Rayden asked for the whole story, so he's gonna get it."

Pretending to be a bit of a prude, Jay jerked his head towards Rob and said, "Oh, brother, you're not gonna tell them that!"

Rob laughed. "Oh, why not—like they don't already know?"

"Oh, go ahead," Jay laughed.

"You guys know, I've been accused of hassling your pore ole dad on a *rare* occasion or two over the years, and so, like I just told him, you also know exactly what I'm talking about when it comes to Maddie's petting zone. But, Grossman didn't, so, I had to explain the whole thing. I told him when Jay and Madelyn are dancing to some slow song in the living room with the drapes closed, instead of wrapping her arms around his neck, she slips her hands into his back pockets. She *claims* the petting movement we all see is her keeping time to the music. So, then I told him, if he believed her line about that one, I wanted to talk to him about a little investment proposal he might like.

"Like all of you are doing right now, Mr. Grossman couldn't help but smile before telling me he thought he'd pass on that *wonderful* opportunity.

"So, anyway, that's when I sprung my extra-extra credit scheme. I told Grossman, 'Um, by the way, I might have another haiku that I could share with the class which describes the petting zone scenario, if, that is, I can get another ten points extra credit. I need it worse than he does, I said, poking my thumb in Jay's direction.'

"It really was funny because your dad yelled at me, 'What are you talking about?'

Rob looked around the table at his family as they all laughed. "You know what, boys? Before right then, Jay didn't even know about my secret, second haiku. Much to my delight, Grossman said, 'I'm in. Let's hear it'.

"So, I handed him my written copy, stood up in front of the class, and pretending to be dancing with my arms wrapped around some girl's back, and with a soft melodic voice, I cooed haiku number two."

Right then, Rob pushed back his chair, stood, sporting a goofy smirk on his face, and again wrapped his arms around an imaginary dancing partner. With his hands pointed straight down, patting the air in rhythm with his dance, he chanted his extra-extra credit haiku,

SWAYIN' TO THE SONG
SHE SNEAKED HER HANDS DOWN HIS BACK
AND JAY'S 'HEART' WENT **BONG!**

As everyone in the family laughed hysterically, clapping, and slapping the table, Grandma stood up, pushed back her chair, and headed for the kitchen. She looked back over her shoulder and said, "Somebody come give me a hand with the pies. Sunday dinner is OVER."

***

Laughing, William Watson, Sr. looked around the table at everyone else who had also burst into laughter. It sure had been an interesting couple of months—a fantastic beginning with his new-found, combined family. He wondered how many of them had also found closure for one thing or the other during this short time. He couldn't wait until he and Mom Roberts had lunch again the next day to talk more about it. He loved hearing her view on the weird events of the family's past. His biggest hope was that things would never change.

The End

If you enjoyed, *Finding Closure*, take a look at these:

I Can and I Will— is Book 1 of a series of three. This was a twenty year prequel to *Tell Me Why*.

The football team had just finished the last day of tryouts, and the roster sheets had been posted on the door. Jayden, who had played halfback as a freshman, did not see his name on the JV roster. Devastated, he sat alone on the bench in the dressing room, with his head buried between his knees. His mind flashed back to what his father had preached to him his whole life. "You can't do that, you're too puny. You can't do that, you're not smart enough. You *Can't* do that!"

So, what should he do? Should he give up, or should he fight? With the help of a number of people—his teachers, his counselor, his coach, his soon-to-be best friend and his friend's mother, Jayden developed his own life's mantra—I Can, and I *Will*!

Tell Me Why is Book 2 of the series. This comes twenty years after *I Can and I Will*.

Reading the obituary, naming his father as a dead man's estranged son, left Ryan speechless. Who was this man, and why hadn't he and his brother Rayden ever even heard of him? Because of this incident, the boys come to realize they know nothing of their father's childhood. Why? Therein lies the title, *Tell Me Why*.

When growing up in a happy, stable home, sometimes one never thinks of oddities. For the Miller boys, the fact that their last names and those of their grandmother and dad's brother were different never occurred to them. That's just the way it always had been. Sometimes, a jarring episode changes things.

On Monday morning, one of Ryan's friends walked up to him before school and offered condolences over the loss of his grandfather. Ryan had no idea what the boy was talking about. Their family had eaten dinner with his grandpa the night before. His friend said his mother had showed him the obituary that morning, and he should check it out with the school counselor who always carried the daily paper in his pocket. Ryan raced to the front of the school and found the man leaning against the wall chatting with other teachers as the kids entered the building. Mr. Martin took him to his office and showed him the obituary. The questions started there.

Sometimes Home Ain't... "Home Sweet Home"

When Dr. Jack Jackson takes a turn for the worse in the hospital's critical care wing, the nurses notify the family. One of those gathered around is his son, Dr. Jason Jackson, who bemoans the fact that even now in the year 2053 modern medicine can't do everything. Regardless of the sophistication of the time, nature always prevails.

As Jason stares out the window, his mind drifts back forty years to 2013. That's when it all started for him. The first eleven years of his life had been a period of extreme abuse and cruelty. For the most part, he'd been able to block it from his memory over the years. Watching his dad sink farther and farther into the beyond, it all comes back to him in vivid, unwanted, painful detail.

Damey & Grandpa Tutor

Gathered with his adoptive white great uncles for the official reading of Grandpa's will, Damey's mind drifted back fourteen years.

Moving into a Habitat for Humanity's home across from William (Bill) Berkley, a retired secondary school teacher, turned into the first good break in Damey's life. Bill stepped in to be his tutor, mentor, friend, confidant, and eventual adoptive grandpa.

African American Damey and Alex, his Hispanic buddy, teamed up for games and adventures—including the time where the two found themselves lost in the woods after following a pure white deer. One cannot stay lost for long before nature calls. Damey cleaned himself using green, three-pronged leaves found in the woods—poison ivy. Sometimes, RediCares do not concern themselves with patient modesty.

Later in the year, Xavier, Damey's biological father, returned to the scene. Their initial contact left Damey suspicious and not liking him. Shaundra, his mother, had fallen in love with the man at fourteen and wanted to pursue the relationship to see if her lingering feelings were real or imaginary. After Xavier visited a week in April, Shaundra and Damey drove to Oklahoma for two weeks to continue the journey.

Damey and Xavier's relationship deteriorated to the point where he slapped the boy hard enough to bounce him off the cupboards and into a heap on the floor. Using Googled maps, Damey decided to ride a bike back to Michigan—almost 1100 miles.

Damey & the Z-Team

A freakish disaster at sea on an icebreaker left Damey locked in the bowels of the ship with no electricity, water, or heat. The rest of the ship suffered the same conditions with outdoor temperatures ranging in the vicinity of twenty below zero. They, however, were not locked into their rooms.

The US Navy had discovered a mysterious flow of oil seeping out from under the ice shelf in the Antarctic. As a fifty year international ban went into effect in 1988 regarding any oil or mineral exploration in that area of the world, the discovery was automatically suspicious.

For some reason, unknown to Dewline Robotics Engineering, the National Security Administration and Department of Defense were aware of the nuclear powered, oil-sniffing, underwater robot that Damey and his crew had been developing. The NSA contacted the company and asked for help.

As the vice president of Dewline, Dr. Damarian Williams, PhD, AKA Damey, is considered one of the top, if not THE top robotics scientist/engineer "Geek" in the country. Therefore, Sam Wardwell, owner of Dewline, always left all emergency troubleshooting operations up to him, much to the chagrin of his wife, Zandy, and children, Zack, Zaiden, and Zane. The boys hated having Dad gone for extended periods.

As Life Goes On

A teen and young adult paranormal coming of age adventure

While mowing the lawn, Jeremy has an intuitive flash of a hit-and-run accident killing Scott, his lifelong neighbor and best friend. The reality of the accident leaves him devastated beyond belief. He finds no relief until he visits the cemetery for the first time a week after the funeral. When he arrives, he sees a ghost boy, Scott, along with the ghost of Mooshy, his long dead dog sitting on the mound of dirt waiting for him.

After initially freaking out, Scott calms him down and reveals that because of the closeness the two of them have had throughout their lives, his guardian has given them the opportunity to try to discover exactly happened and why.

The two boys set out on a series of teen paranormal adventures attempting to solve the mystery. Once they consider that the case is closed in their own minds, it is time for Scott to leave for good. However, he tells Jeremy that all he has to do is call for him, and he will be able to come if the situation warrants it. As life goes on for Jeremy, he bumbles his way through adolescence—parties, sex, and booze problems.

Suddenly, Marty Johnson, Jeremy's new friend and classmate, disappears for no apparent reason. Marty, who suffers from child abuse and neglect, lives with a step father, Bruno Bashore, who is mean and unstable. Jeremy calls in Scott and together they unravel Marty's problem—saving his life and momentarily, at least, getting Bruno out of his life.

For ordering Kindle or paperback versions, the easiest way is to go here: www.larrywebb-author.com
Or at my Amazon author page here:
https://www.amazon.com/Larry-Webb/e/B007O9BP86/ref=dbs_p_ebk_rwt_abau

Made in the USA
Lexington, KY
30 June 2019